"Speaking of N[...]

"Yeah?" She was alm[...] [...]thering herself back into her self-contained shell again.

"I told him we'd have fish and chips on the beach tonight," Angus said. "Would you like to join us?"

It was as if a clam, opened with caution, had suddenly sensed peril. The shell slammed shut.

"Thank you but no."

"Can I ask why not?"

"Because it's taken me years to accept that I don't need people," Freya whispered. "I just…don't need anyone. So you, Noah and Seaweed are very welcome to share my garden, and I hope you have a wonderful time on the beach tonight. But I'll stay where I belong."

"Alone?"

"I spent years being terrified of being alone," she told him. "And I've spent many more learning that it's far, far better than the alternative."

Dear Reader,

Once upon a time a group of us managed to rent a stunning beach house, a huge rambling homestead set in gorgeous gardens, with tracks leading down to a wonderful swimming beach. We stayed for a week and left with every one of us thinking how wonderful it would be to live in such a dreamy house.

But on our last day as everyone left, I wandered through the empty rooms and thought how it would be to live in such a place alone. Actually maybe not so great?

Which brings me to Freya, who lives in the place of her dreams, with the ghosts of her past as her only company. So what does she need? A hero, of course. Plus a kid? Plus a dog? Plus a whole island of people who care? Bring it on! I had such fun bringing my empty house to life, and I hope you enjoy it, too.

This is the second of my Birding Isles novels. Gannet Island was the first—*Mistletoe Kiss with the Heart Doctor*. This romance is set on Shearwater Island, and my romance set on Sandpiper Island is on its way.

Marion Lennox

FALLING FOR HIS
ISLAND NURSE

———

MARION LENNOX

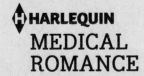

HARLEQUIN

MEDICAL
ROMANCE

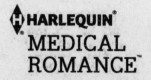

HARLEQUIN®
MEDICAL
ROMANCE™

Recycling programs
for this product may
not exist in your area.

ISBN-13: 978-1-335-40442-8

Falling for His Island Nurse

Copyright © 2021 by Marion Lennox

For questions and comments about the quality of this book,
please contact us at CustomerService@Harlequin.com.

Harlequin Enterprises ULC
22 Adelaide St. West, 40th Floor
Toronto, Ontario M5H 4E3, Canada
www.Harlequin.com

Printed in U.S.A.

Marion Lennox has written over one hundred romance novels, and is published in over one hundred countries and thirty languages. Her international awards include the prestigious RITA® Award (twice!) and the *RT Book Reviews* Career Achievement Award for "a body of work which makes us laugh and teaches us about love." Marion adores her family, her kayak, her dog and lying on the beach with a book someone else has written. Heaven!

Books by Marion Lennox

Harlequin Medical Romance

Bondi Bay Heroes
Finding His Wife, Finding a Son

Falling for Her Wounded Hero
Reunited with Her Surgeon Prince
The Baby They Longed For
Second Chance with Her Island Doc
Rescued by the Single Dad Doc
Pregnant Midwife on His Doorstep
Mistletoe Kiss with the Heart Doctor

Harlequin Romance

Stranded with the Secret Billionaire
The Billionaire's Christmas Baby
English Lord on Her Doorstep
Cinderella and the Billionaire

Visit the Author Profile page
at Harlequin.com for more titles.

In this difficult year, this book might well not have happened without the cheerful companionship of Rusty. My grateful thanks go to Seona, and of course to Audrey and Murphy. You've brought our family joy.

**Praise for
Marion Lennox**

"What an entertaining, fast-paced, emotionally-charged read Ms. Lennox has delivered in this book…. The way this story started had me hooked immediately."
—*Harlequin Junkie* on *The Baby They Longed For*

CHAPTER ONE

'DOG.'

It was the first word Noah had said since they'd boarded the ferry. That wasn't unusual—kids with Down's syndrome were often slow to speak. Four-year-old Noah's big dark eyes seemed to take everything in, but he seldom chatted.

And today there was so much to take in. Two days ago Dr Angus Knox and his son Noah had flown to the Birding Isles to start what Angus hoped would be a new and peaceful life. Angus's new job was to be that of family doctor on Shearwater Island, one of the six islands that made up the Birding group.

They'd come nine months ago, at Christmas, for Angus to talk to the medical staff at the central Gannet Island hospital about possible employment, but there'd been divorce and custody issues to sort before they could come permanently. Now they'd flown here to stay. There'd been two nights on Gannet first, getting to know the regional set-up. Then the nurse who ran Shearwater's tiny clinic—Freya Mayberry—had come to collect them. They were now on the ferry heading to their new home.

Freya was a nurse practitioner, extra training allowing her to perform some of the emergency functions usually handled by doctors. Angus had seen her credentials and been impressed, but on a personal level she seemed almost as uncommunicative as Noah.

His first impression had been that she was cute. Yeah, that was inappropriate, but there it was. The résumé he'd seen had her age at twenty-seven, but apart from her slightly shadowed eyes she didn't look that old. She was five feet two or so, wiry and tanned. Her burnt copper hair was cropped into an elfin haircut, which accentuated wide green eyes, neatly spaced. Her nose was liberally freckled. As a nurse travelling to Gannet to meet the doctor she'd be working with from now on, she might have been expected to dress relatively professionally, but she'd obviously not read that manual. She was wearing denim shorts, a sleeveless shirt tied at the waist, and flip-flops.

So she didn't look professional, but in her conversation she was nothing but. Her answers to his questions were brief, their conversation all about work and very much one way.

Why? Did she resent him coming? That might

be a worry, as it seemed they'd be sharing a house for the foreseeable future.

Then… 'Dog,' Noah said again, and pointed, and Angus stopped thinking about the cute but curt nurse and followed the direction of Noah's finger.

To what looked like some floating debris, a dark brown mass.

They were currently sitting on a bench on the ferry's back deck—the sole passengers of the twenty-person boat. It was a special ferry-run, organised to take just the three passengers plus medical equipment. Now there'd be a doctor on the island, the aim was to equip a tiny hospital. Angus had been told a hall was being converted, and the equipment had arrived almost as he had.

So on board were desks, chairs, a couple of hospital beds, and boxes and boxes of basic equipment. The plan was that he and Freya could now take care of the minor stuff themselves, or do basic emergency work before evacuation to the bigger medical centre on Gannet Island. Or, in worst-case scenarios, evacuation to Sydney.

This meant that right now they were seated behind the mass of boxes loaded onto the back deck. The ferry-boat captain and the boat hand were upfront.

His little son was still staring intently out to the side, to that brown blob floating in the water.

Was it a dog?

'It's some rubbish, Noah,' Angus told him. It looked like a floating bit of nothing. 'Or maybe seaweed.'

But the woman beside him was suddenly on her feet, shading her eyes.

'No.' It was a curt snap. 'He's right. It just moved. Gareth!' She was kicking off her flip-flops, yelling to the ferry skipper. 'I'm going overboard,' she announced. 'Haul to and wait.'

And before Angus could begin to react, she'd climbed onto her seat, taken a fleeting moment to check out the floating blob again—and dived overboard.

It was done so fast they were all left stunned. The skipper, Gareth, a bearded guy in his forties, swore and shoved the engine into neutral. The boat hand, a kid of about seventeen, gave a whoop of excitement and leaped to the roof of the cabin to see.

'Get to the rear and put down the swim platform,' Gareth snapped at him, but Angus was already on it.

He knew boats. He'd grown up with them on Sydney harbour. His parents had had a luxury cruiser they'd used for entertainment. The platform at the back of his parents' boat was set up to be lowered so guests could swim off the boat and re-board with ease.

The ferry's platform looked as if it was used more to help load cargo than to swim from— maybe the flat-bottom boat could be backed into a beach? It was easy enough to slip the catch and hit the winch, all the while watching the slip of a girl streak across the bay towards the…dog?

He was yet to be convinced it was one. She could be risking her life for a piece of refuse.

Actually she wasn't exactly risking her life, he conceded. They were at the entrance to the wide bay that led to Shearwater Harbour. The water was deep and clear, and it wasn't so rough that an experienced swimmer couldn't cope.

And she was an experienced swimmer. There was no doubting that, he thought, as he watched her streamlined figure slice through the swell towards her goal.

Noah was clutching his hand, tight, fearful. 'Dog,' he said again, and Angus swung him up in his arms so he could see.

But was that wise? Maybe he should take him down into the cabin, he thought. If indeed it was a dog, there was every chance that it was already dead. Dragging the body of a dead dog aboard would not be pretty.

She'd said she'd seen it move. That could be wave action. It could…heaven help them…be something feeding on a carcass.

A shark?

He should get Noah out of here.

He couldn't take his eyes off her.

Girl and boat were floating further apart.

'Get closer,' he found himself yelling, and the ferry captain stopped staring in bemusement and turned back to his controls. There was another sharp command to the boat hand, which Angus didn't hear—he was too focussed on what was happening in the water.

'Get dog,' Noah whispered, each syllable an effort, and he hugged him tighter.

'We don't know yet,' he told him. 'It might not be a dog.'

For Noah's sake he should retreat, but he couldn't tear his eyes from what was going on. Part of him wanted to be overboard as well, helping her, but there was no one to hold Noah. He could only watch.

But what to tell Noah if…?

'She's got it.' He could see it for himself, but Gareth's shout confirmed it. 'It *is* a dog.' The skipper slipped the boat into low gear, heading towards them, but he went slowly, slightly off course.

He wouldn't want the wash, or even the propeller, hitting them.

The dog was alive. As Angus watched, Freya touched it, and he saw the mass of floating fur twist and struggle. And claw desperately towards its rescuer.

Once upon a time, Angus had had a golden retriever. Buddy had been a fantastic teenage companion, but she'd been loyal to the point of stupidity. When Angus went surfing with his mates, Buddy was fully convinced he'd drown, and if he didn't have her secured, she'd race into the shallows to save him.

And when she reached him she'd cling. The first time it had happened he'd been twelve years old, skinny and slight, and Buddy was big. He'd been pushed under the water over and over again. Luckily he'd had mates who'd swum to help, but he still remembered the sensation of being weighed down by the lump of panicking dog.

He saw what was happening now and the memory flooded back. The dog was fighting to grip onto Freya. It'd be terrified. Desperate.

The boat hand had clambered down to the back of the boat, a bit late to let down the platform. He was standing gaping at the girl in the water. They were twenty metres or so away, and Gareth had cut the engine.

Angus had been introduced to the deck hand when they'd boarded. Mike was a big, gentle lad who had been gruffly nice to Noah, and Angus blessed him for it now.

'Noah, I need to help the lady with the dog,' he

told him. 'Will you stay with Mike?' And before either of them could protest—this was too important for protests—he thrust Noah into Mike's arms, kicked off his shoes and pants.

Fast.

'You a decent swimmer, Doc?' the skipper yelled back to Angus. He was still behind the wheel, watching Freya and the dog, but also aware of what was going on behind him.

'Yes.' No room for false modesty.

'Then go. Mike, chuck the lifebuoys over the side. They're on ropes. Drag one with you, Doc. Get Freya holding one of them and we'll take over.'

'Done,' he snapped, and then he was over the side, grabbing the first lifebuoy Mike threw and towing it out to whatever was waiting for him.

She hadn't thought this through.

She'd expected a half-dead dog, and that was what she had. It had been totally limp as she approached, apart from its nose, which surfaced every moment or so to gulp in air. It looked as if it was at the end of its strength—maybe even the end of its life.

It was mostly submerged, a mass of sodden black and brown fur. If Noah hadn't pointed, if she hadn't seen that faint movement, she would have taken it for some floating seaweed.

She'd acted on instinct, but if she'd stopped to think she'd have said she was expecting to grab a collar or a chunk of fur and tow it back to the boat. Which would have been easy. As an island kid she'd spent her childhood in and out of the water. Someone had even taught her the basics of saving someone from drowning, how to grab a frantic swimmer.

Not a frantic dog.

And that was an omission, because the moment she touched it, the dog reacted with a surge of adrenalin so fierce she was almost subsumed.

Who knew how long it had been in the water? Who knew how close to death it was? Regardless, one touch and the dog reacted as if it were suddenly in reach of dry land. It grabbed and clawed, and it did so with every ounce of strength left in its body.

This was a big dog, shaggy, huge. She'd only seen maybe a tenth of it above water, like the tip of an iceberg. Two massive, clawed paws found purchase on her shoulders and pushed her under.

She grabbed its feet, trying to break the grip. She did for a moment, managing to surface, and then the dog lunged again.

'No!' She screamed it but the dog was too far gone to register. Maybe if she'd been this animal she'd have lunged at anything within reach as well. She fought to back away, but the dog surged again.

And then stopped, mid surge. Caught from behind.

The dog was trying to twist, still trying to reach her, but it was being pulled further back.

A lifebuoy was thrust sideways across at her.

'Grab!' It was the guy from the boat. The new doctor. Angus. She hadn't seen him come, but he was holding the dog back, fighting to restrain him, throwing curt orders at her.

She grabbed the lifebuoy. The dog couldn't reach her. She took three gulping breaths and the panic eased.

He was still holding the dog from behind, gripping like a vice. The dog had its head above water. Its paws were still flailing but weakly in front of him. There was nothing there to cling to.

'Are you okay?' he demanded.

'F-fine.' Sort of.

How to help? But even as she thought it, her orders came, firm and sure. He'd know that she'd been held under, but he'd figure by the strength of her response, maybe by the sight of her initial swim, that she could still help. 'Hold your buoy and grab me another,' he instructed. 'Mike's thrown three into the water.'

She looked around, wildly.

'To your left. Five metres. Go.' His voice was harsh, loud, totally domineering.

She cast one last glance at the guy practically hidden behind the dog—and she went.

In the end it was almost straightforward. She reached the second roped lifebuoy and swam sidestroke back to man and dog, hauling the buoys beside her. 'Come from behind me,' he told her as she neared, and she did.

He grabbed the second buoy and swung it in front of the dog. Instinctively it clawed and clung, as if it was trying to haul itself onto the solid ring.

'Now you grab my shirt from behind and hold tight,' he told her. 'Don't let go of your lifebuoy. We need the flotation and we need it as backup.'

She was beyond arguing. She grabbed a handful of his shirt and clung.

They were a train. Dog, then Angus, then Freya.

Freya had no use for domineering men—well, not usually. Right now he was welcome to domineer all he liked.

'Pull us in with the rope from the buoy the dog's on,' Angus yelled at the ferry skipper, and finally, clinging to Angus and to her buoy, Freya had a chance to see the overall picture.

Back on the ferry, the skipper had abandoned the wheel. The ferry was drifting, not an immediate risk when they were in the relatively calm waters of the wide bay entrance. The boat hand was holding Noah, both open-mouthed, shocked. The skipper was clambering down to the platform, to carefully, slowly, haul in the buoys.

Amazingly the plan made sense. If the dog let go of the buoy it was holding, Freya was clinging to Angus and she had the extra lifebuoy. Gareth could just swap the lines to pull them in. This way though, the dog's flailing claws were still attached and chances were it would keep cling. All she had to do was hold Angus, and their little procession would be hauled aboard.

When she'd read about this doctor on social media, she'd suspected he might be a waste of space. Maybe she needed to rethink?

What a change. Two minutes ago the dog had been making every effort to drown her and she was fighting for her life. Now she was thinking about the merits of Shearwater Island's new doctor? Gareth was pulling them in slowly—he'd realise jerking the line might have the dog release its hold—so she had time to consider.

Also to feel.

She had one arm hooked about the lifebuoy but her hands were linked under his arms, holding him close. The sodden cotton of his shirt didn't begin to disguise his toned muscles, the breadth of his shoulders—the fact that he was very, very male.

She felt weird. Rescued. Out of control.

But out of control was something Freya Mayberry had no intention of feeling. It broke every rule in her book. And especially for this guy?

When she'd been told Shearwater Island was finally about to get a doctor she'd checked him out online. Of course she had, and what she'd found had left her appalled.

She'd found his basic qualifications, and his years of working as a family doctor in one of Sydney's most prestigious harbourside suburbs. But it seemed as if he hadn't been working very hard. She'd looked up his clinic hours. Five half days a week.

She'd met many part-time doctors during training, doctors who put other interests before their medicine. Some of them had solid reasons, but in this case social media said otherwise.

He personally hadn't seemed to bother with social media much, but he'd been linked over and over to the postings of his wife. She'd seen society event after society event. Pictures of harbourside parties, events on luxury yachts on the harbour itself.

She'd seen a couple of shots of a child in the background, his face blurred, as many protective parents displayed their kids. She'd seen a gorgeous wife.

She knew judging someone by social media was a dangerous pastime, but this guy was going to be so important to her life. She'd followed the trail with increasing dismay.

Something had happened to the marriage, she assumed. This guy would be coming here to save face. Or regroup? Something.

And she was clinging to him.

'I can let go if I want to,' she muttered to herself.

'Don't you dare,' Angus muttered back, and to her horror she realised she'd said the words aloud. 'Just keep on holding on, lady.'

'I'm not a lady.'

'You feel like one to me.' To her astonishment she heard a note of laughter in his voice. She gasped. She was holding him too tight. Her breasts were squashed against his back. Her shirt was too thin and so was his. Of all the...

'We're getting close. Just keep hanging on,' Angus told her, and she had to shove away inappropriate thoughts and focus.

Finally they reached the platform, and Gareth leaned down and grabbed the dog's collar. Angus heaved from behind and the dog slithered upward, collapsing in a tangled heap of sodden fur.

'Help Freya,' Angus told Gareth. He swung

around in the water and grabbed her, propelling her forward.

'I can...'

'I know you can, but you don't have to,' he said, and then Gareth was leaning down to grasp her hands and Angus was behind her pushing her up, and somehow she was out of the water as well.

'Sit,' Angus ordered from the water. And it seemed there was no choice. Her legs suddenly buckled, and she slumped onto the platform beside the dog.

Triage. Medical imperative. She should check the dog's breathing. She should...

She did nothing. The strength she'd had in the water had now drained out of her. She sat, feeling useless, as Angus hauled himself out of the water and headed straight for her.

'The dog...'

'Yeah,' he said, ignoring the dog completely. He'd have his priorities too, she realised, and triage would say women and children first. Before dog? Of course before dog. 'Could you have breathed in any water?'

He'd be checking for water in her lungs. She made herself think back to that first sickening lunge as the dog dragged her down. She'd been caught under its big body but she thought she'd managed to hold her breath.

'I'm okay,' she told him, trying to stop shaking. 'But the dog... Please check it's all right. I'm darned if I've gone to all that trouble to see it die now.'

'Yeah, and I'm darned if I've gone to all that trouble to see you die as well,' he said grimly. 'Gareth, my bag's under the bench on the back deck. Can you grab it for me?'

He was soaked, wearing only boxers and a torn shirt—had she done that? He squatted beside her on the deck, taking his stethoscope from his bag, listening to her breathing, then putting his hand on her shoulder in a gesture of reassurance. He was all doctor.

And his touch... It should have meant nothing, but weirdly it did. It was a warm, firm grasp, a hold that somehow made her body seem to relax. The trembling eased.

Cured by one touch of the stethoscope and one grasp of the shoulder? She had an absurd urge to laugh.

Which would have been hysterical. More nonsense.

'Your lungs sound clear,' Angus was saying. 'But let's lay you on your side.'

'I can help. The dog...'

'I can look after the dog. Gareth, can you find something to put under Freya's head? Freya, lie still until you get your breath back.'

She had enough sense to submit. Yes, she'd

been pushed under, and yes, she'd been terrified. But Angus had rescued her, and now she needed to stay out of his way.

Gareth was edging a towel under her head, offering her another. Fussing at the edges.

She let him fuss. She lay on her side and watched as this new strange doctor headed over to treat the dog.

It had retched. A lot. Poor thing. 'Gareth,' Angus said, and Gareth stopped fussing around her and looked to see what Angus needed.

This inter-island ferry was brand-new, but Gareth was an ex-fisherman, and seasickness was something fishermen often dealt with. One glance and he grabbed a hose and neatly sluiced the mess over the rail—which left Angus a clear place to work.

The dog was breathing. She could see its great chest heaving, surely faster than it should but reassuringly deeply.

Angus put his stethoscope on its chest and listened, and grunted satisfaction.

'He'll live. Throwing up's the best thing he can do. Hey, fella…' Rid of his stomach full of seawater, the dog had now lifted his head and was starting to struggle. 'It's okay, mate. Gareth, do you have more towels?'

He was handed a bundle. 'More where that came from, mate,' the skipper said, and watched as Angus started roughly towelling, using strong strokes that would both reassure the dog and maybe stir up anything else that needed to be got rid of.

'Hey, Skip.' It was Mike. He was still holding Noah. They'd been watching from the deck, looking down in fascination. However, Mike wasn't quite as slow as his open-mouthed astonishment suggested, and the boat was drifting. 'Coming a bit close to the point,' he warned, and Gareth glanced around, swore and headed back to the wheelhouse.

'Dog,' Noah said again, before the noise of the restarting engine meant they couldn't hear him.

'Miss Mayberry saved him,' Angus said. 'Thanks for looking after Noah, Mike. Is it okay if you hold him for a bit longer? Noah, will you stay with Mike while I look after the dog?'

'Yes,' Noah said, and the boat hand grinned and firmed his hold.

'Then let's go up front and get the ropes ready for landing,' Mike told the little boy. They disappeared, and Freya was left lying on the ramp with Angus and the dog.

This was like an emergency ward in a hospital, she thought suddenly, reaction starting to kick in. Two patients, one physician. She gave a choke of laughter and Angus looked at her in concern.

'You okay?'

'I'm thinking,' she managed. 'Up on deck we have hospital beds, monitoring equipment, everything we need for a well-stocked casualty department. If you could unpack fast—and maybe find yourself a white coat—we could lie here happily for a lot more than the five minutes we have left before landing.'

He smiled, but only briefly. 'I don't want any more than five minutes. I'd like an X-ray of your lungs.'

'The X-ray equipment's already on the island, but I don't need it.' With the drama behind her she was starting to feel euphoric. 'I'm fine. One, two gulps of water at most, it can't have been any more than that.'

'I watched you. He held you down.'

'And you saved me.' Her smile faded. 'Thank you.'

'It was a stupid thing to do. If you'd waited we could have got the boat around and hauled him in.'

'With him panicking? You know how close to death he was.'

'Okay, you might have saved his life, but it was still stupid.'

'No, because I got saved in return and that was very nice.' She was still lying on her side, her head cushioned by Gareth's towels. The sun was on her face. She was warm, relief was cutting in and she was watching Angus towel the dog with appreciation.

He was a big man. His wet shirt was clinging to a broad, toned body. He had a tanned face, strong bone structure, deep grey eyes and dark hair that looked a bit bleached at the ends, as if he spent plenty of time in the sun.

He could have been one of the surfers who frequented the surf beach at the tip of the island, she thought. Only he was older. His CV said he was thirty-six, and he looked it. His eyes were creased at the edges—life lines? Was there a hint of grey in his hair?

He looked a bit…battered.

He couldn't be, she thought, remembering the pictures she'd seen on social media. He was a society darling, son of old money—yeah, okay, she'd delved a bit more than was appropriate, but she *was* going to live with him.

And that brought her up with a jolt. She was going to live with this man!

Sort of.

It had seemed so sensible when all the planning had taken place. A month ago she'd received a call from the head of the Birding Isles' medical group and senior doctor on Gannet Island. 'We've had an offer from a doctor interested in starting a medical service on Shearwater,' he'd told her. 'He came to check us out a few months back, and now it seems he's ready to take on a permanent position. If you agree we'll move heaven and earth to get equipment over to you, but he'll need somewhere to live. Your place is close to the clinic, and you've set up the back of your place as self-contained accommodation for tourists. You reckon you could put this fella up until he can organise a place of his own?'

She was so astonished—a doctor for Shearwater!—that she'd said yes before she'd even thought it through. A doctor!

The population of Shearwater was tiny, but medical emergencies still happened, and she'd lost count of the occasions when she'd felt professionally helpless. As the only nurse on the island she was the go-to in emergencies. She could get backup from Gannet Island but that took time, and there were occasions when time meant consequences too horrible to recall.

Having a doctor living in the back part of the rambling house her grandmother had left her would mean he'd be right there. Apparently he'd done additional training in emergency medicine, emergency surgery. That meant in a crisis they could even operate—she could give a competent anaesthetic. In the event of something like the car crash that had happened three weeks back, or last summer when a jet ski had ploughed into a group of swimmers…a doctor on the island would have made all the difference…

Her 'yes' was a given.

Even later, when she'd found his obnoxious social-media presence, she'd still thought her yes was non-negotiable.

The knowledge that he was bringing his son had made her flinch—the thought of a child living in her house left her feeling shaky—but she'd talked herself around that, too. Lily Simons was a neighbour, a kindly grandma whose only son had moved off the island, and she'd jumped at the idea of a possible babysitting job. Freya told herself she wouldn't have anything to do with childcare. The door between the two halves of the house could stay firmly closed.

Problem sorted.

Until now. She hadn't factored in…*this*. Looking at Angus talking softly to the big dog, his hands firm and sure with the towel, his body stooped over while he worked, his clothes clinging…

Down, girl, she told herself and thought, are you out of your mind? You must have swallowed more seawater than you thought for your head to be heading where it's going!

This man was a doctor taking a break from what she assumed was a failed marriage. She'd seen the sudden cut off from Deborah Knox's posts where she'd stopped referring to 'my husband', and the fact that he was now here with his son spoke volumes. He was a socialite from Sydney. He'd only be here as some sort of recovery exercise.

So she did not need to be lying here in the sun letting her eyes dwell on what was, to be honest, a really sexy body.

She did not need to be thinking...what she was thinking...about a guy who was about to be her lodger.

'Just relax until we land,' Angus advised. 'You've had a shock. Close your eyes and treat yourself as a patient for a bit.'

As his patient.

A doctor/patient relationship. She could do that for now, she decided, and after that it'd be a doctor/nurse relationship. Purely professional.

She had no choice. She lay back and tried to close her eyes but her eyes didn't want to close.

Her stomach hurt. She must have twisted something as she fought to control the dog. She winced and he saw.

'What's wrong?'

'Nothing,' she managed. 'Just a niggle in my side—I suspect I've pulled a muscle.'

'Hardly surprising.' He gave her a searching look. 'How bad?'

'Nothing. A niggle. Promise.'

'We'll check it out later.'

'No need.'

'Mmm...' he said, non-committal, and went back to towelling the dog. He was still murmuring gentle reassurances. She wouldn't mind him talking to her like that...

Um, not. Close those eyes, she ordered herself, but it didn't work.

He carried on, and she tried to pretend she wasn't watching.

Then she thought, Why even bother to pretend? Some things were just too hard.

CHAPTER TWO

THE FERRY PULLED up at the Shearwater jetty five minutes later, and Angus had his first view of the place he hoped to live.

It looked amazing.

The bay they'd entered to approach the harbour was huge and shallow. The ferry had had to slow. 'You need to know your way through here,' Mike had told him as he'd handed Noah back over. 'Skip knows the way, but things shift. There are sandbanks all over the place and you can't see 'em at high tide. Skip uses the depth sounder, but I need to look out as well.'

He could understand why. The bay was a sheet of sapphire, glistening in the late morning sun. A couple of the sandbanks were still above water, stretches of washed sand with wading birds of every description foraging for food. As they neared the jetty he saw a cluster of buildings nestled into the foothills of the mountains beyond, and the mountains themselves stretched skyward, wild and free.

Wild and free. He'd read that in the tourist information he'd checked when he'd applied for the job, and he'd seen it for himself when he'd made the quick trip to Gannet last year to sound this place out. The phrase still resonated.

Wild… He ached for that, though he wasn't sure why.

His family had always been city based. The country was somewhere you went for a weekend to try some on-trend restaurant, or if you felt like a weekend on the ski slopes. That had been his parents' world, so of course it had been his too.

During his med training he'd broken away a bit, done some trekking, some hiking. Only then he'd met Deborah, an interior designer with an international reputation. She was a little older than him and a whole lot more sophisticated. Looking back, he could hardly believe how besotted he'd been, and how quickly he'd wanted to marry her.

But their marriage had been Deborah's marriage, he thought. His parents were 'old money' with just the right connections, and Deborah had used those connections as a glossy addition to her career strategy. His career—as a family doctor—had amused her a little. 'Why work with those dreadful people when you don't need to?' But she'd indulged him, and he'd gone along with it.

Until Noah was born…

Don't go there. Think back to that phrase… *Wild and free.*

Shearwater Island was certainly untamed. Its only town was a small settlement on the edge of what was a vast national park, with farmland tucked at the edges. He'd have all the wilderness he could possibly want.

But free?

He held Noah's hand and thought of what free really meant to him. Of what Deborah would have considered free.

'What do you think?' Freya had climbed up to the back deck and come to stand beside him. She was still barefooted. Her clothes were wet, and her short damp curls were clinging wetly to her forehead.

A professional colleague? Not so much.

Distracted, he forced himself back to her question. She'd obviously seen him gazing out over the island. What did he think? Bemused, he said the first thing that came into his head.

'I was thinking my ex-wife would have turned around and headed straight back to Sydney.'

And her reply was prompt. 'My ex-husband would have done the same.'

It was said almost to herself, and the moment she said it he saw her react with shock. Even horror. 'Sorry,' she said, stammering a little as she got the word out. 'I didn't mean… I mean, sorry, that's nothing to do with you.'

'Of course it's not,' he said gently.

He got why she was horrified. He hadn't been two minutes out from separating from Deborah before he'd found himself in a whole new social sphere. Women who, while he was married, would have chatted as friends, now found subtle and not so subtle ways of telling him that they, too, were available.

They usually did it blatantly though, and they certainly didn't back away with a look that warned him to keep his distance.

'So how's the pain in your side?' he asked, deciding the best way forward was to move back to impersonal medicine. 'How are you feeling?'

'Fine,' she said and then decided to be truthful. 'I'm still a bit wobbly.'

'There's a medical diagnosis. Define wobbly.'

He saw her pull herself together and become professional as well. 'No cough,' she told him. 'The twinge in my side's eased. No ill effects except feeling a bit shaky, but that'll just be reaction.'

'You did good, Freya.'

'I nearly killed us both. Gareth could have changed course. Diving over the side like that…'

'Was instinctive. You obviously love animals.'

'Drowning ones?' She shrugged. 'Yeah, I'm a sucker for a cause.'

She was trying to make light of it. A drowning dog was a cause?

He looked down to where the dog was still lying. He'd looped a cord around its fancy crimson collar before he'd come up to reclaim Noah, thinking he should prevent the dog attempting another swim, but there was no way the dog was thinking of doing any such thing. He was lying like a great soggy doormat. Done.

'I guess this guy is a cause,' he told Freya, and she followed the direction of his gaze and nodded.

'Dumped dogs definitely are.'

'You think he'll have been dumped?'

'Probably,' she told him. 'We've had that before. We have yachts coming in here, Americans, Europeans, Russians, usually wealthy, cruising in luxury across to Australia. Scenario is it's a long way. They get bored on the journey over and think a puppy might alleviate the boredom, so they buy a pup while they're in Australia. As they cruise the east coast the puppy grows. By the time they start the first leg of the voyage home, the pup will be half grown and destructive. There'll be hassles of toilet training on the boat, and then there's the realisation that dropping into international ports, coping with quarantine regulations on the way home, is going to be complicated.

We've had a few dogs like that dumped on the island, but the problem is that people see, and our police take a dim view. Solution? Dump it overboard when no one's watching. Tell yourself it can swim to shore and someone will take it in. Problem solved.'

'You're kidding.'

'I wish I was,' she said bleakly. 'People are…' She stopped. 'Well, some people. Not all. And this one will get cared for.'

'How?' he asked, cautiously.

'Gareth will take it back to Gannet on his return trip. There's a woman there—Doris. She takes in injured animals, does her best to fix them and find them homes.'

'It seems a bit harsh to leave him on the ferry now though,' he said with a frown. 'He needs a decent check-up, a feed, a bit of TLC.'

'Doris will give him all that.'

'How long before the ferry returns?'

'It goes back this evening. Four o'clock.'

'That's five more hours on the boat.'

'Gareth will look after him.'

'And if he has water on his lungs? He needs…'

'I don't care,' she said flatly. 'I can't care. Doris will fix him.'

The words were stark, flat, definite.

They were approaching the dock now. Mike was at the bow, readying to step across to the wharf with the stay ropes. Gareth was manoeuvring the ferry towards its berth. The crew of a fishing boat was unloading scallops, heaving crates from deck to wharf. Noah was fascinated.

Normally Angus would be fascinated too, but his attention was riveted on the woman beside him.

I can't care. Where had that come from?

The words had been said almost desperately, as if she was arguing with herself and this was the culmination. The clincher.

'But you want to care?' he asked slowly, and she blinked and he watched her almost visibly haul herself back into a self-contained shell.

'No.' She shrugged. 'Sorry. I'm the only medic on the island, you see, so injured anything gets brought to me. But I'm not a vet and I have my limits. If I kept every injured creature that's been brought to my clinic I'd be running a wildlife sanctuary, not a nursing clinic.'

'Do you have any pets?'

She was still staring down at the dog, and a muscle in her face twisted. Once again he had the impression she was struggling to retreat to her shell. 'No,' she said grimly. 'I told you, I can't care.'

There was that word again. *Can't.*

But then the boat was tied and it was time to disembark. 'We'll get someone to haul all the gear up to your place later this afternoon,' Gareth promised.

But the dog was still on the platform, lifting its head a little and then lying back down, as if it was too much effort.

'Can you take him back to Doris?' Freya asked Gareth. 'I'll ring her and tell her to expect him. I'll also get Pete from the general store to bring down a bit of dog food. If you could give him a little—not too much at a time—and keep fresh water close until you get back to Gannet…'

'Mike and I are heading over the other side of the island to watch the game until it's time to re-board,' Gareth told her. 'Manchester United versus Liverpool. Mike's cousin has a big screen and the replay's just come through. Half the island will be there. The dog'll be right on its own, no?'

'No,' Angus said quietly, and then Noah looked up at them. Had he caught the gist of what was being talked about?

'Dog,' he said.

As if on cue the animal raised its head again, but this time he looked up at them. It was a seriously big dog, black and brown. A near full-grown pup. Shaggy.

It looked straight at them, its huge eyes blank. Expecting nothing?

'It looks like a Bernese Mountain Dog,' Freya said, gazing down at it. 'I bet I'm right. It would have made an adorable puppy, but as a companion on a luxury yacht…' She winced. 'People make me sick.'

'Because they don't care,' Angus said flatly, and Freya cast him a look of dislike.

'Don't do that to me.'

'What?'

'I've lost count of the number of animals islanders have tried guilting me into keeping—just because I have a big garden and I live alone. It's not going to happen.' She sighed. 'Okay, I'll stay with the dog until the ferry leaves, but that's it. My home is mine and I don't share.'

'Yet you're sharing it with Noah and me.'

'Under sufferance,' she said and then caught herself. 'No. Sorry. That was uncalled for, and it's not true. We're all incredibly grateful that Shearwater's getting a doctor. I don't know how much you've been told, but my house used to belong to my grandparents. It's huge and it's now subdivided into two separate residences. I let out the back one and that's yours so I'm not sharing at all. And that includes this dog. I know what'll happen. If I crack and take it home now I'll only have to bring it back to the ferry later, and it'll look at me with those soulful eyes and I'll feel dreadful.'

'They do that, dogs,' he agreed, and he looked down again at the dog. 'A Bernese Mountain Dog, huh?'

'Adolescent. It still has growing to do.'

'You know dogs?'

'I might not be a vet, but until you arrived I've been the closest approximation to one the islanders have had. So yes, I know dogs. No one on the island has one of these, though. They wouldn't be so stupid.'

'Why?'

'It'll eat like a horse. It'll shed by the bucketload. If I was weak enough to take it home it'd take up three quarters of my living room.'

'Weak?'

'Yes, weak,' she said stiffly. 'I'm not a soft option.'

No, you're not, he thought as he watched her. But she *had* offered to stay with the dog until Gareth returned to take the ferry back to Gannet. If she was indeed responsible for every medical emergency on the island, if she was the go-to for every stray animal then okay, he got it.

But as he looked at the big dog, as he considered the lowlife who'd bought a cute puppy and then tossed it overboard when it outgrew its cuteness, he also thought...this was his new life. Why not start as he meant to go on?

Not every stray, but one might just work.

'What about *my* living room?' he asked.

She frowned. 'What?'

'You heard.'

'Dog,' said Noah, and beamed, as if he'd indeed been following the gist of this conversation and was pleased with its progress.

'Exactly,' Angus said, and swung the little boy into his arms and hugged.

His wife had had Siamese cats, a matching pair that had spent their lives sitting in the sun in the bay window of their perfect home. They'd been just the right decorator touch. Noah had learned early that approaching them meant hissing and scratches. Deborah's reaction was to ban Noah from the living room.

He thought of Deborah's reaction to this mass of soggy fur, and he could almost hear her incredulity. 'Get that thing out of here!'

But he wasn't in the market for decorator items. This wasn't your run-of-the-mill, normal pet dog but...well, nothing needed to be perfect any more.

Or hidden.

'Let's take him home,' he told Noah, hugging his son tighter. 'The doggy's sick but we'll try and make him better. Then, tomorrow, we'll ask him if he'd like to stay. If he doesn't like little boys, if he can't be gentle, then we'll find somewhere else for him to live, but let's ask him first. That is, if our landlady agrees. How about it, Ms Mayberry?'

'Call me Freya,' she said shortly. 'But you're out of your mind.'

'I don't think I am.'

'Your son...'

'Comes first,' he agreed. 'So if it doesn't work then we'll find another way, but we'd like to try. Wouldn't we, Noah?'

'You realise if he's unsuitable you can't just shove him through the dividing door and leave him to me?'

'I wouldn't do that. Freya, this dog will be my responsibility. You want me to sign something before I take him?'

'No,' she said slowly.

'Then trust me.'

'Why should I?' She seemed to catch herself then. She shrugged and even managed a wry smile. 'You don't know what you're letting yourself in for, but I'll sit on the fence for a bit. Meanwhile you'll need to shop on the way home. If there's a football game happening, the general store will be locked within half an hour. I've stocked your apartment with provisions but not dog food, dog beds, leads and bowls. Your apartment comes with a stick vacuum and that's not going to cut it. I hope the store stocks an industrial-type sucker because you'll need it.'

'A sucker...'

'I'm thinking the dog's already found one,' she told him, and for the first time her face relaxed into a grin. 'So, unless you want to drown in dog hair, it's up to you to find another.'

CHAPTER THREE

'Dog. Toast. Dog!'

There was nothing like being climbed on by a four-year-old to wake a man.

Angus emerged from sleep regretting how long he'd stayed up the night before. He'd spent the evening unpacking, reading the raft of information Freya had given him about current and potential medical services on the island—and sitting with the dog.

He'd done a thorough examination and found no reason for further treatment, but the dog's shock had seemed profound. He'd encouraged him to eat and drink, and then decided quiet might be the best medicine. They'd settled him in the laundry on a bed of old towels and he'd slept, which had given Noah and Angus time to explore their new home. It was only towards midnight that the dog had stirred and started to howl. It had taken Angus a couple of hours sitting, stroking, talking softly, until he'd finally settled.

He wasn't howling now, though, and here was

Noah, aching to start the day. And why wouldn't he? Tiredness aside, Angus was pretty excited himself.

The house seemed great. It was huge, perched on a hill overlooking the sea, with verandas all around and a garden that left him stunned. There were lawns that looked perfect for a kid—and dog—to play on. They could glimpse the sea wherever they turned.

The garden was fenced, but simply, with posts and wire so there seemed little boundary between private land and the gorgeous sweep down to the beach. Paths meandered through a seeming wilderness of semi-tropical plants, but as he and Noah explored he'd realised that wilderness was the wrong word. Such beauty could surely never happen by accident.

And the house itself… They only had one side of the rambling homestead, but it was more than enough. The rooms were generous, with timber floors that looked as if they'd been polished by a hundred years of use, comfortable furniture, faded rugs. French windows looked out over the garden to the sea beyond, and grape vines looped under the veranda.

'There's a track down to the beach at the end of the garden,' Freya had told him and pointed out a key on the ring she'd given him. 'It's gated. When I knew a child was coming I fitted a lock.'

She'd thought of everything. The kitchen was stocked with food for a week. The fireplace was set and ready to light.

'I've also asked one of our neighbours—Lily Simons—to pop in and meet you late tomorrow morning,' she'd said diffidently. 'We can change that if you want, but I thought you'd be needing childcare. Lily's lovely and she lives only two minutes down the lane, but she'll understand if you want to make your own arrangements.'

'Does she look after dogs, too?' he'd asked, and Freya had given him a strange look and laid the keys on the kitchen bench with what was almost a slap.

'You'll need to ask her. That's it, then. You have my phone number if there's anything else you need.'

'Could I not just knock on the dividing door?'

'I'd rather you didn't,' she'd said curtly. 'We'll keep ourselves separate, Dr Knox.'

'I would like to check your lungs,' he'd said, thinking of her lying on the boat, thinking of water on her chest, but she'd shaken her head.

'No need. I just produced a very fine yodel in the shower, and if I can do that there's not a snowball's chance in a bushfire that anything's wrong.'

She'd walked back through the dividing door, he'd heard the key turn in the lock—she hadn't given him *that* key—and that was that.

Home.

So he and Noah had explored to their heart's content and he'd felt more and more hopeful that he'd done the right thing. Noah had snuggled happily into his new bed. Angus had spent the evening unpacking, checking on the dog, reading, then trying to shush the dog's howling...and trying not to think about the woman next door.

Who had him seriously intrigued. What had she said on the boat? *'I can't care...'* There was a story there.

Which wasn't his business, he'd told himself as he'd finally drifted to sleep. Nor was the vision he had of her yodelling in the shower. That was inappropriate. He managed to block it—so why the thought of her should be front and centre in his mind the moment Noah climbed into his bed the next morning made no sense at all.

'Toast,' the little boy said now. He clambered up and settled beside him with satisfaction. 'Good,' he added, sounding happy, and that made Angus's grin widen.

'It is good,' he said and hugged his small son and then a howl echoed through the house that could have woken the dead.

Or the landlady in the other side of the house.

'Dog?' Noah said, but Angus was already out of bed heading for the laundry. The dog would have kept his landlady awake last night and he didn't want to push his luck further.

They opened the laundry door to find him on his feet, wobbling a little, staring at the back door rather than the inner door. As he heard the door open he turned and looked at them with such a look of desperation that Angus almost laughed. Message received.

'Toast?' Noah said helpfully, but Angus opened the door and the dog headed unsteadily out to the lawn.

'He needs the bathroom first,' he told Noah, which Noah found confusing. He stared at the dog and then looked back into the house towards the bathroom.

'I mean he needs to pee. Dogs pee on the grass,' Angus told him. And the rest. He went back to the kitchen to find a plastic bag, thinking wistfully of the neat litter trays Deborah had set up for her cats—even of the housekeeper she'd insisted they hire when they were married. 'We can't combine two careers without hired help,' she'd decreed and so there'd been a housekeeper and then au pairs to help with Noah. Emptying litter trays was therefore never in their family orbit.

But now, as they followed the shaky dog into the morning sunshine, where Noah watched the process of dog toileting in awed fascination—

how could anyone ever have thought they could have handled that on a yacht?—Angus thought everything was in their orbit.

Toast forgotten, they rambled across the lawns. Their bare toes were wet from the damp grass. Noah clutched his hand and the dog sniffed behind.

The poor animal must have spent most of its short life on a boat, Angus thought. He was sniffing and snuffling in delight as if he couldn't believe where he was—and Angus was feeling much the same.

Then they rounded a corner and Freya was sitting on a garden seat. A trellis of scented apricot roses formed an arch above her head. She was wearing faded pyjamas and a loose, open kimono and she looked…amazing. 'Hey,' she said, smiling at Noah. Not smiling at him… That was a dumb thing to think, but there it was. 'Good morning.'

'Poo,' Noah said and nodded decisively at Angus's bag.

Freya grinned. Her short-cropped curls were tousled, as if she'd just woken. A loose belt at her waist held a pouch with a phone, but the rest of her spoke of a woman at peace.

'We'll need to find you some compostable bags,' she said, looking at what he was carrying.

'Bags,' Noah said, not comprehending but

game. He walked up to the bench and hitched himself up to sit beside her. 'Sit,' he said, meaning himself, but to everyone's astonishment the dog sat.

'Wow, good training,' Freya said, and her eyes lifted to his. He saw laughter. She looked relaxed, he thought.

More. She looked beautiful.

'Yeah, we've been training all night,' he told her. 'You want to see him catch a frisbee from fifty paces?'

'Indeed I do. Was that what you and he were talking about at two this morning?'

'That was us setting down ground rules,' he said, and the laughter deepened.

'Go you. So you're keeping him?'

'He seems to like Noah,' he said, as if in explanation. The fact that the big dog had looked at him all the time he'd examined him the day before, the way those huge eyes had followed him with what looked like hope and trust... The despair of that howl in the night...

Yeah, he was keeping him.

'How are you feeling?' he asked. 'No cough? No after-effects?'

'None at all,' she assured him. 'And I haven't even been landed with a stray dog, so I've escaped scot-free. What are you calling him?'

'Seaweed,' he said, because at some stage yes-

terday he and Noah had discussed it and decided
it was satisfactory. 'Because that's what I thought
he was. It was only you and Noah who saw the
dog underneath.' He glanced again at the roses
cascading from the arch above her head. 'This is
one fabulous rose.'

'It's called Scent from Heaven,' she said, and
flushed a little. 'Scent as in perfume.'

'Got it,' he said. 'You wouldn't want a rose with
a soppy name.'

She smiled at that, but he thought she looked
a bit strained.

'This looks very much like your spot,' he told
her. 'We don't want to intrude. Should we divide
the garden?'

'No.' She rose—ready to leave?—and he was
aware of a stab of disappointment. 'I have thought
of fencing off a part for myself—you know I've
been using your place as a holiday rental?—but
the garden is so great even I think it should be
shared.'

'Even you?'

'You might have figured by now that I keep to
myself,' she told him. 'But out here I reckon I'm
okay.' And then she bit her lip as she heard what
she'd said. 'Sorry. That sounds silly but there it is.
The garden is to be shared and you're welcome.'

She was okay in the garden? It was a jarring

term, one that made him wonder just what was behind the façade.

Did he want to find out?

Um, not. He was just emerging from a disastrous marriage. This woman clearly had a lot of baggage, and he had enough of his own.

But still, he didn't want to go inside, and he didn't want her to go either. Not yet.

And maybe neither did she. Freya had stood but she was now hesitating, watching Noah and Seaweed. The morning sun was warm. Seaweed had abandoned sitting and had edged forward to stand beside Noah. The little boy was snuggling his head against Seaweed's soft ears and chuckling as the dog's hair tickled his nose.

It wasn't a bad place to be.

What sort of understatement was that? It seemed like heaven, and the sight of this woman under her roses… Wow, she was lovely.

He was regretting that he was in his sleeping gear—boxers, T-shirt and bare feet. But then, maybe that made things informal, and he had a sense that given a more formal setting she'd retreat back into the shell he'd glimpsed yesterday.

'So who does the garden?' he asked, because it seemed the most neutral thing he could think of.

'Me.'

He gazed around at the 'lawns', which on further inspection he'd discovered to be tracts planted with some sort of soft ground cover, with wildflowers peeping through. At the amazing flower beds, with masses of colour. At the trees shading just where they needed to shade, trees that were alive with birds of all shapes and sizes. His parents had had a garden as big as this and they'd employed a full-time gardener.

'You and whose army?' he asked and that brought a wry smile.

'Just me. It's not as labour intensive as it looks—it's designed to be more natural than manicured. And it wasn't me who designed it. This was my grandparents' house, and my great-grandparents' before them. My great-grandma and my grandma were both fanatic gardeners. I must have inherited their green thumbs.'

Her great-grandmother and her grandmother. He heard the omission. 'Not your mother's?'

'Not my mother's,' she said, a bit too quickly. 'Mum had multiple sclerosis, and from the time I first remember she was ill. She died when I was ten, so most of what I know I inherited from Grandma. I... I let this place go for a while. It's been a struggle to bring it back, but it's worth it.' She turned and gazed out to sea. 'It has to be worth it.'

'Toast,' Noah said, suddenly remembering what was important, but Angus looked at Freya for a moment longer, sensing her fold herself back into her shell. Noah was ready to move on and, it seemed, so was she.

This was not a good time to ask questions that were suddenly front and centre. They were questions he had no business asking anyway.

'Good idea,' he told Noah. 'Toast.' And then for some unknown reason he added to Freya, 'Care to join us?'

It was a mistake. The shell slammed shut.

'No,' she said bluntly. 'The garden yes, because it'd be too selfish not to, but everything else… Not. Dr Knox, we have our separate homes and that's the way I like it. So thank you for the invitation but I don't share. I've organised Lily to be here later on to meet you and see if you're interested. Jake from the garage will be delivering the car you organised this morning as well. So make yourself at home. Tomorrow I'll show you the clinic and we'll start from there.'

'Why not today?'

'You need today to sort things out, and so do I. Did you see the amount of gear that arrived on the boat with us yesterday?'

'Unpacking our gear's not a big deal,' he told her. 'If Lily's happy to stay on and Noah's content, then maybe we can sort it out together for a couple of hours this afternoon.'

'If you wish,' she said stiffly, 'but I can cope by myself.'

'The doctors on Gannet Island said you've been coping by yourself for too long. All the medical needs of the island, plus this garden…'

'I like to stay busy,' she said, still stiff. 'So I'm moving on. Right now I need my breakfast, so I'll leave you to get used to your new home.'

'I think it's going to be perfect.'

'That's great,' she said, and turned and left. Without smiling.

She didn't bolt back to the house. She made herself walk slowly, conscious that he might be watching.

She was sensing that she'd let him see more than she was comfortable with, and she was kicking herself. She needed a professional relationship with this man and nothing else.

It was surely only that Noah and Seaweed had touched a nerve. The sight of the little boy coming out into the garden, hand in hand with his dad…

As if on cue a spasm hit her gut, a stab of pain that might have caused her to pause and catch her breath if she hadn't been so conscious of walking steadily towards her side of the house.

It's stress, she told herself. She'd had a gut ache ever since she'd found out her new tenant would be a guy with a little boy. A child only a little older than…

Don't go there.

She was already there, though, the familiar pain enfolding her like a heavy grey blanket. She should be over it by now, she told herself—but how many times had she said it, and how many more had she realised that such scolds were useless?

Moving on. Breakfast. She walked inside and put bread in the toaster and looked out to see Angus and Noah walking back to the house. Noah was giggling. Seaweed was following gamely behind. He was still a bit staggery—he was far too thin for such a big dog, she thought. Maybe she could ring Doris for some advice. Doris's schtick was sick animals. She'd know what to do.

But maybe she should give Angus Doris's number and let him ring her instead, she told herself, turning deliberately away from the little group outside. Or she could just leave the whole thing to Angus. He was a doctor. He could surely decide whether a dog needed supplementary feeding or not.

A doctor. Here. There was a thought to distract her from the all too domestic sight of this little family. And she needed to be distracted. There were far too many personal emotions being stirred within.

So…work. There was so much to do. She glanced at the whiteboard she'd fixed to her kitchen wall when this extension to the Birding Isles medical service had been proposed. First there'd been a tentative outline—find a doctor, then figure the logistics of setting up a clinic for two-bed overnight care. The plan was that with a doctor on the island they could provide emergency hospital care for occasions when the weather was too wild to evacuate to Gannet Island. Also they'd set up a tiny theatre for emergency procedures.

The board then had been uncluttered, a broad plan. Now it was covered with minute detail, and there were sheaves of notes clipped beside it.

The islanders had already worked their butts off, refitting the ancient scout hall to turn it into a tiny hospital. The bulk of the gear had arrived yesterday, and now it all had to be unpacked. Flat-pack beds could be put together and sorted by the locals, but organising the medical equipment was down to her.

Angus had a little boy to familiarise with his new surroundings. He had a dog to care for. He had a childminder to meet and a car to organise. That was plenty to keep him occupied.

And she'd have a whole day without him. A day to let herself settle.

So why was she unsettled?

To her annoyance she found herself thinking of the little group on the lawn again.

She'd had families stay here before—of course she had. The back of the house had been rented out for holiday accommodation for two years now, so she'd already shared her garden with parents, with children, with dogs. And Angus was a doctor! Shearwater Island was desperate for a decent medical service. She should be totally focussed on that.

She was…sort of.

This unsettled feeling was because he wasn't in the least what she'd expected, but she'd expected…what, exactly?

He was a wealthy city doctor. She'd figured he'd come from a failed marriage. She'd been told he was bringing a child.

Shearwater Island was almost as remote an outpost of Australia as it was possible to find. Sydney was their closest city but it was over an hour's flight, and by boat it took days. Lots of visitors to the island had baggage—failed marriages, trauma. They came here to escape, to lick their wounds until they could return to the mainstream.

So she'd been expecting a doctor who'd soon miss the lights of Sydney. She knew from her social-media pages that there was nothing wrong with Angus's ex-wife. This must therefore be a separation, if not a divorce. Noah's mother must want some sort of access to her son, she thought, so Angus would need to be going back and forth to the mainland as often as he could. Eventually for ever?

That was okay. Any doctor was better than none, and if Shearwater became the base for a series of temporary doctors that was a far better situation than the one she'd been coping with for years.

So that was what she'd been expecting—maybe it still was—but other factors had now come into play.

Noah. Down's syndrome.

The little boy was obviously struggling with language. Down's syndrome meant he was physically a bit awkward, with little of the lithe grace of most pre-schoolers, but every sign said this was a little boy who'd been cherished.

There was an adult on the island with Down's, Robbie Veitch, now in his early forties. His dad had died early, his mother had been overwhelmed with caring for her two small children on a pittance of an income, and there'd been little attention to his special needs. The islanders looked out for him with casual kindness, but he wasn't safe left alone—he wandered and there'd been times when the whole island had had to search for him. Even now he struggled with language, struggled to understand simple instructions.

Every time Freya saw him she regretted the missed opportunities of his childhood. His mum did the best she could, but she was failing herself now, and when Freya had returned to the island and tried to get involved, his sister had bluntly refused any offer to assess, or even help him. 'Don't bother with Robbie,' she'd said bluntly. 'He's a waste of space.' The casual cruelty, the dismissal of any possibility of having help had made her cringe.

But here...

Freya had done enough mother-child training to recognise that Noah had been stimulated, worked with intensively from birth. And the way he clutched his dad's hand...the way he chortled... The way Angus looked at him and how the little boy nestled against him with total trust... It was enough to twist anyone's heart.

And then of course there was the dog, blithely accepted as a long-term acquisition.

She thought once more of his ex-wife's social-media pages, and figured there was no way a child with Down's syndrome would fit the absent socialite's image. Nor would a vast, lanky and ultimately unfashionable dog.

So here was a guy committed to a small child with Down's. A doctor who'd calmly taken on the care of a dog that threatened to end up as big as a small horse.

A man who'd gazed around him this morning with an expression of absolute peace. Like someone who'd come home.

She thought back to her initial judgement when she'd read the social-media feeds. He'd only worked half-days, and she'd jumped to a swift assumption, thinking of golfing afternoons, sailing, whatever.

Was it possible she'd misjudged him? Was it possible he'd spent his spare time giving Noah the one-on-one attention he must surely have had to reach his impressive milestones?

She was too ready to rush to making judgements. She knew she was, but it was a way of keeping herself safe. Her appalling marriage, a tragedy she could never get over, had left her permanently mistrustful.

Should she reconsider? Was it possible that Angus was here to stay?

Oh, for heaven's sake… Her toast had popped and had grown cold in the toaster. She was air-dreaming, and air-dreaming was something she had no time for. She ate cold toast and showered and dressed and headed down the hill towards their new makeshift hospital maybe faster than she needed to.

As of tomorrow she'd be working with this guy, and she needed today to get her mind back into some sort of practical order.

So why was it out of order?

It wasn't, she told herself crossly. It couldn't be.

CHAPTER FOUR

LILY ARRIVED JUST after Noah's nap, and the potential childminder was absolutely, gloriously perfect. In her sixties, little, plump and oozing warmth, within minutes she had Noah giggling and Angus grinning as if he'd won the lottery. She'd been introduced to Noah and to Seaweed, and she was now sitting on the floor with both of them, discussing dog biscuits.

'This dog is too skinny,' she told Noah, and Noah looked at her with trust.

'Si…sinny.'

'I used to have a dog called Roger,' Lily told them. 'I made him dog biscuits. He liked ones that looked like cats.'

Noah stared at her in perplexity, and Lily giggled and tugged him onto her knee. She had Seaweed nestled by her side and Angus looked down at the trio and thought this was better than he could ever have imagined.

Freya had done this, he thought. She'd found them…a fairy godmother?

No, just plain Lily, who seemed better than any fairy godmother he could imagine.

'If your dad says it's okay, maybe you could help me make dog biscuits,' Lily was saying. She looked up at Angus and smiled, suddenly a little shy. 'But we can do it as a friend if you don't want to employ me, Dr Knox. As a neighbour. I used to help my husband on his fishing boat, and I was so busy with that, and with raising my son and nursing elderly parents, I've never had a real job. So it doesn't really matter if you want to pay me, but I'd like to help anyway. Making dog biscuits is fun.' She looked around at Angus's pile of half-unpacked boxes. 'We could even do it this afternoon, if Noah agrees, and if you need some time to yourself.'

'I do want to employ you,' Angus said promptly, thinking of the uncommitted au pairs Deborah had serially employed every few months as she'd worried that they'd become too close to the family, that they might gossip to the outside world. *Deborah Knox has a child who's less than perfect...*

'Really?' Lily said, flushing with pleasure, and Angus made an instant decision to increase the salary he'd been going to offer.

'Biscuits,' Noah said firmly, as if the thing was settled, and it was.

Delayed gratification wasn't something Noah appreciated, so ten minutes later Angus watched in bemused wonder as Lily and Noah walked hand in hand down the driveway—*'My house is really close to your front gate'*—with Seaweed following gamely behind. Neither Noah nor Seaweed could quite understand what was happening, but they both seemed happy.

Angus felt pretty much the same.

He had a childminder who Noah already adored. More, Lily had said she was willing to come here at a moment's notice. He had a spare bedroom. She could leave some of her night things here if he'd like, she'd suggested, and she was a light sleeper, so if he was called in the night she could just swap beds. Or he could drop Noah to her if he wanted. She had a little bedroom right next to hers that Noah might like.

This was all said in the diffident tone of one who was aching to be useful, who wanted desperately to be a grandma substitute, and he just knew this woman would make Noah happy.

He watched them go and felt an enormous weight lift from his shoulders.

Freya had said she'd be unpacking the equipment. She hadn't seemed to want help, but this was what he was here for, to help her. The sooner he started, the better.

His new car had been delivered—a sensible SUV organised by the Birding Isles medical group. He could thus drive, but he checked the map Freya had left and decided to walk. The clinic and prospective hospital looked to be just down the hill, a ten-minute walk. Or twenty if he took the cliff path.

Cliff path, he decided. He wanted to take in as much of this island as he could.

It was a good decision. The path was cut into woodland, with bush turkeys scuffling in the undergrowth, lorikeets squawking in the vast eucalypts overhead and lizards scuttling out of his way as he approached. The sea was glimmering below the cliffs.

He was starting to feel like the kids in that book who'd stepped through the wardrobe and discovered a fantasy kingdom behind.

That kingdom had had problems, he told himself, but today he wasn't looking for problems. Sydney with all its heartache seemed very far away. He was Shearwater Island's brand-new doctor, and he could hardly believe his luck.

At the end of this path was his landlady and colleague, setting up the new Shearwater Clinic. Freya.

She wasn't expecting him. Use today to make yourself at home, she'd said, and he should.

He should stroll slowly, but his feet seemed to be moving fast, whether he willed them to or not.

Freya didn't have to cope with setting up beds, desks, computers. The locals had been in last night and done the heavy stuff. For the islanders this new order couldn't happen quickly enough. They'd cleaned up after themselves and removed any packaging. Refitting had been going on for weeks and the place was gleaming.

All it needed was a final sorting of equipment.

And a doctor.

Freya was reading the instructions for the steriliser when he walked in. She hadn't heard him enter and his 'Hi' made her jump.

He was wearing casual chinos and a short-sleeved shirt. His dark hair was faintly ruffled—had he walked here?—and his eyes were crinkling into a smile.

Oh, my…

'Sorry, did I startle you?'

'Yes,' she said, but then thought no, that sounded grumpy. 'It's okay. You're welcome.' Then she thought, Here he is, a real live doctor for Shearwater Island. 'You're very welcome,' she added gruffly, and his crinkly smile deepened.

'I'm glad.'

She fought to make her voice prosaic. Normal. She was confused that she had to struggle to do it. 'By Noah's absence I assume you've met Lily?' she managed.

'Lily and Noah are currently making cat-shaped dog biscuits. Seaweed is supervising. She's wonderful.'

'Isn't she? Her husband died two years ago,

her son and grandkids live in London and she's the kindest, most motherly person I know. If you need a hug, Lily's just the person to give it to you.'

'She gives you hugs?'

'From time to time,' she said, and struggled to find a non-personal example. 'When my hundred-year-old lemon tree died of root rot, she was there for me. What more can I say?'

She got a searching look at that, as if he didn't quite believe her. Or maybe he did; maybe he sensed that dead lemon trees were minor in her hug-requiring life events.

Well, that was nonsense, she told herself briskly. This man knew little about her apart from her professional credentials, and he didn't need to know more.

'So I have a couple of hours free,' he said, and she got the impression that moving on had been a conscious decision. Had he looked at the emotion on her face and decided not to pressure her?

Whoa, she was putting ideas into her own head. Why should he be thinking about her?

'How can I help?' he was saying, and she hauled herself back to practical.

'I told you we didn't need you today. You should be getting to know your new home.'

'Don't make me feel unwanted,' he told her and put on a sad face, and that made her smile again.

'We have the bulk of it sorted,' she conceded, 'but there are still boxes to be unpacked.'

'We?'

'Every single islander wants this place up and running,' she told him. 'I just have to say the word and we'll have a hundred islanders ready to build, scrub, sort, do anything that's needed. I've asked that they leave the medical equipment for me to sort, though.' She stood back and looked around with pride. 'You want to see how this whole place is set up?'

'Yes, please,' he said promptly, and she abandoned unpacking and became tour guide.

One upon a time the islanders had built a scout hall next to the school. Twenty years ago, though, a visiting teacher had introduced the offshoot sea scout movement and the scout hall had been abandoned for meetings on the beach. A new hall-cum-boatshed had then been built, and this building had been unused ever since.

Troya had thus taken it over. When she'd returned to the island the locals had fitted out rooms at the back for consulting and examination. The rest of the hall had been spare space but the last few weeks had seen it transformed.

She led Angus through and couldn't suppress the thrill of satisfaction. Even excitement. There were now cubicles that, with the newly arrived equipment, looked like two hospital rooms.

Screens gave privacy, but they could be rolled back, so if only one was in use a partner, parent or friend could spend the night as well.

'We don't see this being used all the time,' Freya explained. 'But there are cases where it'd be safer to keep islanders here rather than evacuate. Now that we have a doctor, if I get a croupy child, or if one of the islanders needs intense medical care during the last few days of their life, I won't...*we* won't need to send them off the island.'

She'd caught herself on the *I* as opposed to *we*. It was hard to get her head around the fact that now there'd be someone to help her.

'If we have inpatients, that means we'd need to stay here,' Angus said thoughtfully, looking around at the comprehensive preparations.

'That's been thought of, too.' She led him on. The end of the hall wasn't where it should be. A door through a walled partition led to an office, then to another curtained partition with a bed.

'If we needed to stay then we can,' she told him. 'That'll mostly be me, with you as backup just up the road. We also have volunteers who'll sit in and wake us when needed—everyone wants to help. We'll still use the local library for things like vaccinations, antenatal classes and so on, but this should give us plenty of room for the day-to-day stuff. So...what do you think?'

He didn't answer. Instead he prowled, heading from cubicle to cubicle, from room to room. He took his time, checking equipment, seemingly taking in every last detail.

'This is amazing. I was told we'd be starting a medical service from scratch. What you've done…'

'It is from scratch,' she insisted. 'We've never had a doctor here, and I can only hope this'll work.'

'You've given it the best shot.' His brow wrinkled as he tried to think of complications. 'You have health department approval? Compliance?'

She motioned to a folder big enough to use as a doorstop for a small castle. 'Howard Ainsley's a retired accountant. He came to live on Shearwater to spend his retirement fishing, but he was only too keen to help. He's been through the health department rulings with a fine-tooth comb and says we have everything sorted. Sarah Goldsworthy has an industrial washer and dryer she uses for the island's footy team. She's happy to do our linen, as well as our cleaning. Ben Cartwright at the pub did an online course on invalid cooking and can't wait to extend his repertoire. I think we're set.'

'You certainly are.'

'You can't imagine how much the islanders want this,' she told him. She hesitated and then added, diffidently, 'You can't imagine how much the islanders want you.'

'No pressure,' he said, and she grinned.

'Okay, no pressure. We know there's a two-month trial period, but you have come here assuring us you want to stay for at least a year.'

'I intend to stay a lot longer than a year.'

'I guess... I hope...'

'You don't think I will?'

'We'll see.' She managed a smile. 'I guess you have a dog now, and once Seaweed's tasted Lily's dog biscuits you may well be stuck for life.' She hesitated. 'It will be different from what you're used to,' she warned. 'It's a long drive to the other side of the island, especially at night. We have oldies who are desperate to stay at home when they become ill, or at least not leave the island. If they need intensive medical care over the last few days of their lives, with you here we can bring them in here. Or in simpler cases...a pneumonia or an infection...a couple of days here will save them trauma and the government the cost of evacuation. Win-win for everyone. But it's not what you might call exciting medicine.'

'Except for sometimes,' he said, watching her face.

'Except for sometimes,' she agreed. He had her disconcerted, the way he watched her. It was as if he was trying to read her, as if he found her a bit puzzling.

And then her phone rang. 'Excuse me,' she said with some relief, and turned away.

She had him fascinated.

He was starting to see it now, this woman's commitment to the island. He thought of Marc, the cardiologist organising the new Gannet Island medical centre, saying, 'We've organised Freya to come across and accompany you back. It'll be a chance to show her the new order of things here. She hasn't been across since we opened. She hasn't had time.'

If she'd been the only medic on Shearwater, it would have even been a risk for her to go to Gannet. Did she ever take holidays? And what was a lone woman doing living in such a vast house?

And now... She had the phone to her ear and her face was losing colour.

'The Travis Road paddock? How far in? It'll take me ten minutes to get there, Sam, so hold tight. Do what you can to clear his airways. Get his mouth as clear as you can and don't take your attention from him for a moment. Tell him I'm on my way.'

She shoved her phone back into its pouch, grabbed a bag from a storage cupboard and headed for the door. 'Tractor accident,' she said curtly. 'Sounds bad.'

'I'm with you.'

'You're not supposed to start work until tomorrow, but thank you.' Her tone held relief but also a note that said it didn't matter what his decision was, she needed to go anyway. She was out of the door, leaving him to follow.

They reached her car, a serviceable, slightly battered red van. She swung into the driver's seat and he was in beside her just as fast.

'Tell me what's happened?'

'Gary Mayberry.' Her voice faltered a little. 'He's my uncle. He has a farm ten minutes from here.' They were travelling along what passed for Shearwater's main street. A car pulled out in front, and she jammed her hand on the horn so hard it could probably be heard all over the island. The car revved back into its parking spot fast. The locals would know Freya's car, he thought, and they'd know that horn meant trouble.

'He's been trying to plough his top paddock for more pasture,' she said briefly. 'It's steep country. I've warned him about fitting a roll bar to his tractor but he's old school, thinks safety gear is for sissies. He's rolled on the slope and is trapped by his leg. Facial injuries. Breathing difficulties.'

She pulled out her phone and tossed it to him, all her attention on the road. 'Can you hit One on the emergency list. It's Donna, our island cop. Tell her we'll need lifting equipment. Then hit Two, the med centre at Gannet. Tell them to send the chopper for evacuation, with a surgeon on board if possible. Someone who can cope with facial injuries. We can always call it off if we don't need it or if...'

Then she braked, hard. They'd rounded a bend to find a farmer walking behind cows plodding along the middle of the road. The window was wound down in an instant. 'Get 'em clear, Doug,' she yelled. 'Gary's rolled his tractor. He's stuck and injured.'

There was a shocked expletive, ending with a shout that sent the cows scattering off the road into bushland. 'I'll get them back later,' the farmer shouted. 'You want me to bring my tractor in case we need to pull?'

'Yeah,' Freya called. 'And can you call Aunty May?' She was already accelerating, but the message had been received. The farmer had abandoned his cows and was starting to run.

Angus's medical practice for the last ten years had been in inner Sydney. As such he'd coped with standard family medicine, skewed slightly because of the upper-income socio-economic area where he lived. Coughs, colds, problems of an aging population, a smattering of neurosis from the worried well, parents fretting about kids, young mums concerned about their babies.

His practice had suited the lifestyle Deborah desperately wanted. Once Noah had arrived he'd had to go part-time, to give his little boy the attention he needed, but it had left him itching for more. His solution had been to use his extra training in Emergency Medicine. Once upon a time, before he'd met Deborah, he'd fancied it as a career choice. He'd started down that road and he'd kept his training current. He'd thus put his name down for extra night shifts at Sydney Central Emergency. He was only called when the department was under pressure, but when that happened, the medicine he practised was a far cry from his normal work.

As was this, field casualty work, but Freya's speed told him she was obviously accustomed. She swerved into the open gateway of the paddock she'd been directed to, and was out of the door practically before the car stopped.

'Go. I'll bring the gear.'

He went.

It took him only seconds to see what had happened. The paddock, almost flat at gate level, rose steeply and flattened again at the top. To plough the sloped area seemed inherently dangerous—even Angus could guess that. Surely such a small area of pasture wasn't worth the risk?

The farmer had obviously decided it was. There was a wide stretch of ploughed land on the lower slope, then a curved furrow where it started to rise. Basic physics made turning tractor on such a slope a major risk. What had happened seemed almost inevitable.

The tractor lay on its side. An elderly man was standing behind it, waving wildly.

'I saw the tractor roll from the road,' the man said as he approached. 'He's stuck. He can't breathe. Doc, he looks awful.'

Angus reached him and looked down and his heart sank. He did indeed look in deathly trouble.

Gary Mayberry was a big man, around fifty, in typical farmer gear of flannel shirt and moleskins. Angus couldn't see his feet. They were somewhere under the tractor. Pinned?

But his legs couldn't be the priority. He must have hit his face as the tractor rolled. It looked a bloodied mess, and even before he reached him Angus could hear his whistling efforts to breathe.

'Geez, Doc, thank God you're here.' The guy who'd waved was practically sobbing in relief. 'He can't talk. His breath's been bubbling. Rattling. Wet. There's so much blood…'

'Got it,' Angus said. It was already known, then, that he was a doctor?

Of course it was, he thought as he knelt. A new doctor arriving on the island would be big news.

Now it was time to justify his existence.

The farmer was conscious, but there was no way he could speak. His face must have been smashed as the tractor rolled. A broken jaw. Broken teeth. A mouth full of blood.

Neck injuries? Spinal injuries? Trapped legs.

Clearing his airway came first. The man's breathing was shallow, fast, ineffective. Weakening. His eyes were rolling in terror. With the amount of facial damage, it looked impossible for him to get enough air into his lungs to survive.

First things first. He cleared as much of the mess from Gary's mouth as he could, then grabbed his hand and held. 'Mate, you're going to be okay. I'm the new island doc, and here comes Freya. We'll fix your breathing, and then fix the rest of you. Doug's coming with his tractor to get you free.' He didn't know Doug's surname but assumed a neighbour would be known. 'Let's get your breathing right and then get you out of here.'

Freya was with him now. 'Oh, God, Uncle Gary, what've you done?' She knelt and touched his bloodied face, just the one touch—and then she looked at Angus.

She got it, he thought. In that one glance he could see comprehension, plus acknowledgement that what they were facing was beyond her. That what happened next was up to him.

He'd seen—and used—this glance in his workplace, time and time again. As a junior doctor handing control to someone who'd been in this situation before. As a doctor standing back to let a trained paramedic cope with the thrashing of someone on drugs. As a doctor ceding authority to a midwife who'd been with the mother even before labour. Authority was handed over in that one glance. Freya was already hauling her kit open, but any decisions were over to him.

'Trachy,' he said, and she flinched, but moved to find what was needed.

Freya was a nurse with specialist training in emergency medicine. The theory of tracheotomies was part of that training, so in theory she knew what to do. In practice, she'd trained on dummies in a nice clean teaching environment. This was about as far from that environment as it was possible to get, and the thought of doing one scared her witless.

More, this was her uncle Gary, a man who'd been there for her for ever.

Oh, thank God Angus was here. The thought of facing this alone…

She didn't have to. She was here as his assistant and she was needed as such.

She was working fast, setting out a waterproof sheet to use as a tray—the best thing she had to keep equipment vaguely sterile. Given the emergency situation, formal sterilisation had to be set aside. Potential infection could be dealt with later.

'Morphine,' Angus said, and she had the syringe in his hand almost before he asked. Then she moved to check blood pressure. Oxygen saturation.

'Ninety systolic,' she murmured. 'Oxygen saturation eighty-five.'

Angus nodded, then gripped Gary's shoulders, needing to talk through his terror. 'Gary, we're making a wee nick in your neck to put a tube in to get your breathing stable. You won't be able to talk after the tube's in, but it'll clear your airway until we can fix the bleeding in your mouth. It's a simple procedure and the moment the tube goes in your breathing will be okay. I promise. Freya here is going to hold your hand tight, and I want you to focus on her hand. I need you to keep very still for me.'

The panic in the man's eyes seemed to recede a little. Here was a positive thing he could do.

She had one hand free to hand equipment over as needed. The other she slipped into Gary's and he grabbed it as if he were drowning.

'Your breathing will be okay. I promise.'

It was a huge promise, one Freya could never have made.

A simple procedure?

Not so much.

'Not gonna watch.' It was the elderly farmer who'd called them. He was backing away, looking sick.

'Can you head over and make sure the gate's wide enough for Doug's tractor to fit through?' Freya asked him. She knew it was, but the old guy had lost colour. The last thing they wanted was for him to collapse.

'Got it,' he said and left at a stumbling run. Now Freya's full attention had to be on what Angus was doing.

She knew the drill. Find the area over the cricothyroid membrane—that'd be the soft spot where the incision would be made. Make a horizontal cut, around a centimetre wide, the same size deep. Make an incision into the membrane itself, just deep enough to gain access to the airway. Place a tube about five centimetres into the trachea.

It sounded easy. It was anything but. One false move…

There was no false move. Angus's fingers were skilled and sure, as if this was…a nothing. Dear God, though, if she'd had to do it…

She watched in stunned silence as Angus performed a textbook procedure, and in moments it was done. With the tube in position he gently breathed into the straw, checking to see if air was coming back, confirming the tube was in the right place.

Gary took a deep breath on his own, and then another. The panic eased from his eyes.

'Hey, all's good,' Angus said, and smiled down at him. He was taping the tube in position, speaking reassuringly as he did so. 'Sorry, mate, you can't talk for a bit. You know you have a few broken teeth?' And the rest, Freya thought, looking at the obviously broken jaw. 'We'll need to evac you out to someone who can make you pretty again, and the tube'll have to stay in place until then. Now, let's get a bit more painkiller on board and see what's happening with your feet.' He glanced across at the gate and saw a tractor speeding in. It was the farmer they'd seen with the cows, with a woman clinging behind him. 'Here comes Gary with the tractor.'

'And Aunty May' Freya added. 'You know she's going to give you heaps for not fitting that roll bar, Uncle Gary.'

Gary rolled his eyes and even managed the faintest glimmer of a smile.

CHAPTER FIVE

GARY'S LEGS WERE not as badly damaged as they'd feared. The tractor had rolled onto newly ploughed dirt. His legs had been pushed downward into soft soil, so the weight of the tractor was dispersed.

Doug's arrival heralded the arrival of others. Donna, the island cop, appeared with a couple of beefy guys she'd brought as backup. It seemed rolled tractors weren't so unusual on the island. While Doug used his tractor to stabilise Gary's, they dug him free.

One of his legs was obviously broken, but in the light of what could have happened he'd been lucky. The chopper from Gannet landed as Angus stabilised the break. Two paramedics plus a surgeon were on the chopper and in minutes Gary and his wife were in the sky, heading for the Gannet Island medical facilities. Doug and Sam left to find Doug's cows. Donna and her guys left to help.

'If they stay wandering until nightfall we'll end up with a car crash,' Donna decreed.

Freya and Angus were left alone.

'You did great,' Freya told him as they watched the police car disappear out of the gate.

'You didn't do too badly yourself.'

'If it was just me here, he would have died.'

'Then it's lucky we're a team,' he told her, and she cast him a look he didn't quite get.

'Let me drive,' he said as they gathered their gear, but she shook her head. She was still pale, clearly shocked.

'I'm fine.' She obviously wasn't, but he didn't argue.

'I'm sorry this had to be your uncle,' he ventured as they headed back to town.

And when she broke the silence she sounded bitter. 'Uncle. Cousin. Friend. It's all the same because I know them all. Every single islander was at my mother's funeral, and why I should remember that every time something happens…' She grimaced. 'Tell me what it's like working in a nice anonymous Sydney clinic.'

'A far cry from this,' he agreed. 'Caring's hard.'

'You're telling me.'

'So why stay?'

'What kind of question is that? Because I do care. I only left the island because I couldn't train as a nurse here.'

'But you married off the island. I gather this place was without any medic until you returned.'

She flashed him a look of resentment. 'How do you know I married off the island?'

'Marc told me. He's the head of Gannet Island—'

'I know Marc,' she snapped. 'His wife's my best friend. So he's been talking about me?'

'You also know it was Marc who offered me the job.' Her anger was probably due to reaction, he thought. 'He was talking about the medical services the island's had in the past. He only gave me the bare facts, that you'd done your training in Sydney, you married, the marriage broke up and you came home again.'

'Yes, I came home,' she said curtly. 'Not like you. A failed marriage with a society princess, and you've run away to recover. We get them all the time here. People who come here escaping from their lives, regrouping before they head back again. They don't stay. I'd be astonished if you stay.'

There was a moment's silence. This had suddenly become personal on so many levels.

He should never have brought up her marriage, he conceded, but the facts he'd been given had seemed impersonal enough.

'Freya's a godsend,' Marc had told him. 'She's a nurse practitioner, and her additional training's enabled her to do basic emergency procedures. Island born. She left to do her training, married, then came home when the marriage broke up. She restored her grandparents' home and is now providing Shearwater Island with the best medical service it's ever had. Basic, but a whole lot better than the nothing that was there before.'

Maybe what Marc had told him had been sensitive information, he mused, but surely it was general knowledge. Whereas his circumstances…

'Society princess?' he said, and she reacted as if he'd slapped her. He could almost see her listening again to what she'd said.

She pulled over to the verge and stared straight ahead. She looked stricken.

It wasn't just her expression. A streak of blood ran from the side of her face into her hair. Her T-shirt and jeans, pristine when he'd seen her at the clinic, now looked like something you'd see on an accident victim rather than a nurse.

He remembered her holding Gary as they'd waited for the chopper. She'd been kneeling beside him, telling him things were going to be okay, the painkillers were kicking in, the tube would make his breathing easier until the doctors on Gannet could patch him up.

It had been a combination of excellent nursing and intuitive care. She'd been murmuring to him, reassuring nothings, verbal assurances that he wasn't alone. And then, as the chopper had readied to leave, her aunt had hugged her as if she were drowning. As Seaweed had tried to hold onto her.

As every islander must sometimes have needed to…

Her uncle's accident was intensely personal to her, he thought, but then…clearly the health of the entire island was intensely personal to her as well.

'I'm sorry,' she whispered, and it sounded as if she was struggling to find her breath. 'That… what I said about your… Deborah…it was unforgivable. You look after Noah… You've taken in Seaweed… And as for you not staying… I've been working on stupid assumptions, ideas I'm already figuring are wrong.'

She'd pulled off the road in an area of bushland. The open windows were letting the sea breeze waft through the car, and from the trees came the sweet, pure notes of the native bellbirds. It was a place of beauty and of peace.

She'd accused him of running away. Maybe she was right. But how did she know about Deborah? For this woman the question was obviously a biggie. Right now she looked as if she'd been caught stealing.

'Society princess?' he asked again, and she flinched.

'I looked,' she said at last. Her hands were

clenching so tightly on the steering wheel her knuckles showed white.

'Where?' he asked, gently now, because any anger had been dispersed by her reaction.

'On social media,' she muttered. 'Totally intrusive. Creepy. Stalking.'

'You searched for information about me online?'

'I'm so sorry. I had no business doing that...'

As an apology it'd take some beating. There was all the regret in the world in her voice.

He knew instinctively that if he'd searched for her profile, he'd have found nothing but bare facts. Even though this woman was such a public figure on the island, he was realising that she valued her privacy above all else. For her to be caught out intruding on his... Okay, he'd cut her some slack.

'Um...social media can be a public forum if you allow it,' he conceded. 'There's no need to apologise. You had a new doctor coming to the island.' It hurt to say it, but he had to be fair. 'Maybe it was even reasonable to search.' Then he frowned. 'But apart from professionally I hardly use social media. How...?'

'Your wife,' she whispered. 'She has links to you all over the place. Search for Dr Angus Knox and there you are. I should never have gone down that rabbit hole, but I did, and I can only apologise.'

Of course. He hadn't followed Deborah's posts, but he could imagine what Freya had seen. He remembered a random colleague coming up to him after he'd returned from their last holiday… 'That's a cracker of a place you stayed in. Biarritz? My wife says that's the trendiest place in France. And that meal… Six stars? Wow, those oysters…'

That had been their final 'family' holiday, but they hadn't been a real family. He remembered sitting on the beach with a contented Noah, but he also remembered Deborah's horror at his suggestion she join them instead of shopping with women she'd met at the resort.

'It was you who insisted Noah come with us,' she'd snapped. 'If you think I want our new friends seeing our precious family… For heaven's sake, Angus, I told you how it would be. At least leave him with the resort babysitter tonight and join us for dinner.'

It'd been anything but a family holiday, but he wasn't about to talk about it now, though.

Because it was humiliating? Because he'd had to concede his marriage had been a failure from the start?

But then he looked across at Freya's white face

and thought what was he doing, letting her feel guilty?

It was Deborah who had secrets, not him. Her social-media presence had been a carefully concocted front. The perfect marriage. The successful husband. The adorable child who was never allowed to be photographed face on to the camera.

Freya would have seen all that, but the family image Deborah had presented to the world had little to do with him, and even less to do with Noah.

'But I bet you never found out Noah has Down's,' he said, a little too roughly, residual anger at Deborah only partly concealed.

She winced. 'No.'

The effects of the accident were still with her, he thought, as he watched her almost visibly regroup. Her reaction of horror would only partly be because he'd discovered she'd researched Deborah's online presence. It was mostly because she'd almost lost her uncle.

He wanted that expression wiped from her face. She looked gutted.

'Well, I guess it's no secret,' he told her. 'I was married, and you're right, Deborah did indeed see herself as a society princess. Our divorce came through six months ago.'

'I'm sorry.'

'You need to stop saying that—but I don't see what I've done as running away. I see it as trying to find what Noah and I need.'

Then, as the look of mortification was still there, he decided to continue. Anything to take that stricken look from her face. 'It was a disastrous marriage,' he admitted. 'I was so caught up in my career and Deborah in hers that we met and married without really knowing each other. Then we had Noah and things fell apart. She couldn't bear that Noah was less than…her version of perfect.'

Finally she looked directly at him, caught by his story. The streak of blood was still on her face, shocking against her pallor. He had an almost irresistible urge to wipe it away.

He didn't. For some reason she was reminding him of a deer caught in headlights. The tough, capable woman he'd met seemed to have disappeared. She looked as if she was hurting. Vulnerable.

Lovely?

There was an inappropriate thought. He'd had it before though. There was something about her…

'She hated that he's Down's? And you?'

How on earth had they got so personal, so fast?

He could make some curt rejoinder. He could tell her the advent of Noah into his life was none of her business—as indeed it wasn't.

But if he was to work beside her—if she was to become his friend, and for some reason that seemed increasingly important—then maybe it was time for truth. For personal to be okay.

And the descriptor was somehow still with him. Lovely.

She wasn't lovely. She was a bit too thin, a bit careworn, a bit…bloodstained.

Why did it seem so important to strengthen the connection between them? To speak the truth.

'It was only Deborah who never wanted Noah,' he said bluntly. 'When he was born she was appalled. For me it was different. I guess from the moment I looked down into his little face, from the first time I held him in my arms, I was hooked.'

Her face changed, emotion taking the place of shock. Good, he thought. And if being personal helped drive away trauma, then why not continue?

He hesitated, tossing in his mind how much to say and then deciding, dammit, why not be honest?

'I wanted kids,' he told her. 'Deborah was ambivalent, but our friends were having babies and that swung things for her. What everyone else had, Deborah had to have. The agreement was that we'd employ carers, though. My career was important to me, and I conceded that hers was to her, as well.'

'That was good of you,' she said wryly, and he shrugged and even smiled. But not with any humour.

'Yeah, okay, I was an arse. Deb and I both come from privileged backgrounds, and we moved with the right people. People with influence. I was building up a great medical practice that saw me treating some of Sydney's finest. I did a bit of emergency medicine when needed—I liked it and was training to take on more—but mostly in my time off I surfed or I studied. Deborah's and my worlds seldom collided, and maybe I didn't realise how little. But then Deborah got pregnant and she didn't tell me.'

She frowned at that, and he had the satisfaction of knowing that, even if his story was hardly a good reflection of his character, for Freya it finally seemed to be driving away the day's events.

'Why not?'

'Because a group of her friends had arranged an extended vacation in Switzerland,' he explained. 'Three months on the ski slopes, plus all the trimmings that went with it. She was desperate to go, but I couldn't—or wouldn't—take three months off. Not that we couldn't afford it, but I was studying for a post-grad exam in emergency medicine and the surfing at home was great. Plus,' he said, deciding to be totally honest, 'snow is really, really cold.'

And that produced a smile. A real smile. A gorgeous smile. He smiled back at her, and wondered why he felt as if he'd won the lottery.

'So?' she prodded. He didn't particularly want to go on, but he didn't want to lose that smile either.

There seemed no choice.

'So Deb realised she was pregnant just as the trip was suggested, and she knew me well enough to know I'd either have made a push for her to stay home, or I'd have gone with her. But I was already starting to cramp her style, and once Deborah wanted something that's what she took. I guess I was lucky she didn't decide to have an abortion before she left, but the desire for a cute little baby to show off to the world was still there. Her pregnancy seemed easy, no illness, nothing to make her slow down. She was three months pregnant when she left.'

'And you didn't even suspect?'

'I was busy,' he told her, regretful. 'And, as I said, we largely lived our own lives. I wasn't even too fussed about her being away for three months. So she went. We were in contact most days, but she's one of these women who carry their babies relatively unobtrusively, and ski clothes are great for hiding bumps. I don't know if any of her friends suspected, but I saw nothing.'

'So she had no tests,' she said slowly.

'I think she just blocked it out. This baby wasn't going to interfere with her life in any way. But then of course she came home. Thirty weeks pregnant. I realised the moment she got off the plane. "Surprise," she said, and my initial reaction was joy. There was shock that she hadn't told me, but I hadn't realised how much I wanted a child until I saw that bump.'

'So,' she said, and it was her turn to sound gentle now.

'So of course I did the doctor thing and insisted on medical checks, and a week later we knew our baby had Down's.'

'What happened then?'

'Deborah just lost it,' he told her bluntly, remembering those awful days. 'She was hysterical, demanding an abortion, but of course it was far too late. And then she just turned off. Noah was born and she wouldn't feed him. I remember bringing them home, carrying Noah into the house and Deborah walking into the bedroom and slamming the door. "You wanted a kid. He's yours," she said. "Or put him in a home. Get him adopted. I don't care."'

'Oh, Angus.'

'Yeah, it's a tough story,' he said. But then he

smiled. 'Not all bad, though, because I had Noah. I kept hoping Deb would come around, and she did, sort of. She built a happy family story for her friends. She referred to me and her baby on social media, but she never referred to his Down's. Only her closest friends knew, and they sympathised with her.'

'I guess—'

'Hey, don't you dare agree with her need for sympathy,' he said, roughly now. 'Okay, at first it took some adjusting, accepting our son would face challenges most kids don't. But he's been amazing right from the start. We had au pairs, but I spent a lot of time with him myself, and I can't tell you how rewarding it's been. How much fun. Down's kids used to be locked away, and what a tragedy that was. They're not tragedies. Often there are underlying health issues. I know Noah's never going to be a brain surgeon, but he has so much potential. Only Deb couldn't… wouldn't see it.'

'That must have been appalling.'

'That's exactly how her reaction was—heart-breaking, in fact—but nothing I could do changed it.'

He should stop now, he thought. He was talking too much, but suddenly the need to explain everything was overwhelming.

'Our marriage became a facade,' he conceded,

'but I was busy and preoccupied, and all I could do was make sure Noah was happy. While he was tiny it became just the way things were. It was only as he grew old enough to understand… things that were said…that I realised that Deb would never stop feeling ashamed of him, that I couldn't protect him from her disgust, and I couldn't let him live with that. So there you are. If running away means giving Noah the best chance for a happy life, and finding him a community who'll accept him for what he is… If that's running away, then I'm guilty as charged.'

'Oh, Angus…'

'Don't say you're sorry again,' he warned. 'Because I'm not. I have a great little son who's going to take to this island like a duck to water—I know it. You seem to have found me a babysitter a step better than Mary Poppins. I have a ready-made pet called Seaweed who threatens to carpet my entire house with his shedding—that'll be a saving on mats. Plus I have a skilled colleague and a workload that, if today's anything to go by, is going to be far more challenging than any job I've ever had before.'

'It won't always be like this.'

'I hope it won't,' he agreed. 'Freya, let's head home and have a shower. I'm filthy.'

'Me, too,' she told him. And then she hesitated. 'But, Angus…'

'Mmm.'

'About me… I did marry off the island.'

'There's no need to tell me.'

'I think there is.' She took a deep breath. 'I don't…ever talk about it. I can't. But today… There was no need for you to tell me what you just did,' she said bluntly. 'As there was no need for me to get my knickers in a knot just because someone told you I'd been married. So tit for tat. I was married. It was a disaster. I lost a baby and I came home.'

Whoa.

Where to take a statement like that? She was back to clenching again with those white knuckles and he knew she was expecting…something.

Sympathy? No. But talking?

I don't ever talk about it. He'd been a family doctor long enough to know such a statement meant that there was a well of pain underneath.

And the way she looked… A part of him was suddenly prompting him to take her into his arms, to ease her pain with the warmth of physical comfort.

He knew instinctively how fast she'd back away.

So…he was a doctor. Go down that path, he told himself. Make it professional.

'You lost your baby,' he prompted, gently,

ready for her to pull back if she wanted to—or needed to.

'Chloe. Born at thirty-four weeks, almost three years ago. She lived for two days.'

'I'm so sorry,' he said, uttering each word with care. 'I can't imagine how dreadful that must have been for you. That still is.'

Something twisted in her face. A stab of pain so deep…

'I can still feel her in my arms,' she said, sounding desperate. 'I held her and held her and yet there was nothing I could do.'

Silence. There was nothing to say to a statement like that except wait, be there, be open to whatever she needed.

The silence stretched on. He'd learned though, after years of family medicine, that silence was often necessary. Consultations were usually booked in fifteen-minute slots. Sometimes silence took most of those. Sometimes fifteen minutes needed to stretch to half an hour or more. The queue in the waiting room would be growing, his receptionist would be becoming desperate—but silence was often the only gift he could give.

And when it stretched to the point where her face changed again, he sensed it and moved forward.

'Your husband?' Two words. She could be about

to tell him of complete tragedy, he thought. Of a car accident and death. Of abandonment.

'He's in jail,' she said, and the words were so shocking they made him flinch.

'In jail?'

'He hurt me. Badly. That was why Chloe was born early, so damaged.' She shrugged, her face expressionless, as if she were passing on patient information instead of something so intensely personal.

'Okay, fast explanation. My mother was a single mum, and when she died I was brought up by my grandma. Grandma died when I was eighteen, just as I was about to leave the island to train as a nurse. I'd hardly been off the island, I was still traumatised by Grandma's death and I met Craig. He was an instructor at college, ten years older than me. I knew no one, and Craig was…well, he seemed wonderful. He took over my life and I let him. He loved that I was little and defenceless, someone he could look after, someone who adored him and hung on his every word. So we married, and I was his devotee, and then…then I grew up. And he didn't like it.'

'Hell…'

'It was in the end,' she said, still in that strange, dispassionate voice. 'I found myself in a place I hated. I spent my life trying to please him and it never worked. When he hit me, somehow it seemed almost reasonable, like I deserved it. He was jealous of any friendship I formed at work and he sabotaged any outside link I made. When I wanted a baby he seemed to like the idea—in retrospect maybe he thought it was something else he could control—but when I got pregnant things got even worse.'

'He still hit you?'

'Harder,' she said bleakly. 'And I was so brainwashed I couldn't get away. In the end, as I started preparing for the baby, it was like a bad dream. Every time I started talking about the baby… every time I showed joy, I realised he couldn't bear it. I was his, and he didn't want to share me. He came home one night after he'd been drinking and I was sitting in our baby's room sorting baby clothes and…' She stopped. 'Well, that was it, really. End of story.'

'Oh, Freya…'

'So that's all there is,' she said, and she took a deep breath and moved on. 'I'm over it now, or sort of. After hospital the doctors referred me to a women's refuge, and I got the help I needed. Counsellors who made me see how brainwashed I'd been. People who helped me understand I could stand on my own two feet. And now I can. I moved on.'

'Except you lost your baby.'

'Craig killed my baby.' She said it flatly. 'The

counsellors already took me down that road, and I get it. I didn't lose Chloe, Craig killed her.' She closed her eyes for a moment, and when she opened them she turned to him and dredged up a smile. 'I wanted Chloe like you wanted Noah. You've come here because of him and that's awesome. Well done.'

'That sounds…' He wasn't quite sure; he was struggling here on so many levels. 'It sounds a bit patronising, actually.'

'No,' she said flatly. 'It's jealousy if you like—you managed to save your baby and I didn't.'

'By pure luck. Deb would have—'

'Don't go there,' she said quickly. 'There's no what ifs. They do your head in.'

'Right,' he said and nodded, feeling his way. With caution. How much of what she'd just told him was public knowledge?

Her next statement answered him. 'And please, don't tell anyone. No one on the island knows about Chloe, and I don't know why I said anything to you.' She was hauling herself together now and he thought, yes, this was her private grief. Told to him because they'd both been under pressure, because he'd revealed his story and somehow it had unlocked her guarded past.

'You can be sure I won't,' he told her. 'As I'd expect you not to talk about my past. I want Noah to grow up thinking his mum's too busy for him, not that she loathes him.'

'So hard for him.'

'The fact that he's Down's will help,' he said simply. 'Noah takes things at face value and I hope he always will. Speaking of Noah...'

'Yeah?' She was almost visibly gathering herself back into her self-contained shell again.

'I told him we'd have fish and chips on the beach tonight,' he said. 'Would you like to join us?'

And it was as if a clam, opened with caution, had suddenly sensed peril. The shell slammed shut.

'Thank you but no.'

'Can I ask why not?'

'Because it's taken me years to accept that I don't need people,' she whispered. 'I just...don't need anyone. So you and Noah and Seaweed are very welcome to share my garden and I hope you have a wonderful time on the beach tonight. But I'll stay where I belong.'

'Alone?'

'I spent years being terrified of being alone,' she told him. 'And I've spent many more years learning that it's far, far better than the alternative.'

She ate a light dinner and took a hot-water bottle to bed, hoping there were no calls in the night. Her stomach hurt.

Well, what was new? She'd had intermittent

stomach cramps since…well, she wasn't going there. The doctors had talked of phantom pain. The counsellors had said of course, what could she expect?

What she had to do to get rid of the pain was to get over the past, stop thinking of it, concentrate on the here and now.

Except today the past had merged into the here and now. What had she been thinking, baring all to a stranger? To a colleague? To a guy who was sharing her house?

Since returning to the island she'd never talked of it. No one knew of the tiny pile of ashes buried by a rose called Scent from Heaven.

Angus might figure it out. If she wasn't careful she might even tell him herself. That she'd opened up to him today was extraordinary. Frightening.

It was getting late but it was still daylight outside. As she lay and hugged her hot-water bottle she heard them return from the beach. Angus, Noah and Seaweed. Angus was singing, some funny kids' song. Noah was giggling. Seaweed was giving the occasional tentative bark, as if the world he'd found himself in might be threatening but he wasn't sure, and maybe he might just give it a go.

She had an almost irresistible urge to get out of bed and peep through the curtains.

He'd see. Of course he'd see, or if he didn't see then he'd probably sense her watching.

'I'm like Seaweed,' she told herself. 'Thinking things might be threatening me but I'm not sure.'

How could things be threatening her?

They weren't, she told herself. The status quo hadn't changed. She'd made a vow when she'd walked out of the women's refuge that she'd never need anyone again.

That vow hadn't changed. She was secure here. Safe.

So why did her stomach still hurt?

CHAPTER SIX

W<small>HEN HE'D BEEN</small> on the island for three weeks she decided she should formally concede he was awesome.

Her workload had halved. Her responsibilities had quartered. When she'd returned to Shearwater and become the island's sole medic she hadn't realised just what a load she'd be taking on, but in the last three weeks she hadn't felt out of control once.

Her uncle rolling his tractor had just been the start of it, she thought, reflecting back as she finished filing the week's paperwork on Friday evening. Her uncle Gary had been helicoptered to Gannet Island where the surgeons had stabilised his tracheotomy and broken leg. He'd then been evacuated to Sydney.

She'd had a phone call from her aunty May this afternoon. His facial reconstruction had gone well and his leg was healing. He was doing brilliantly in rehab and Aunty May was even finding time to enjoy Sydney. The shopping was excellent.

'Please thank Angus.'

Of course she'd thank Angus. She was under no illusions when it came to her skill set. Her uncle would be dead without him.

But as well as emergency traumas there were the smaller imperatives. Geraldine Vine, ninety-six years old with terminal cancer, was currently slipping peacefully from life in the big front room of her daughter's house. Freya had been at her wits' end to stop her from suffering, but nothing she'd tried was helping. She'd been about to recommend that for all their sakes it'd be better if Geraldine could be sent to the hospital on Gannet. A palliative care specialist could ease her passing, even if it meant she had to die off her beloved island.

Angus, though, had changed everything. He had the skills, plus insight into how much the old lady wanted to stay where she was. He'd tried different medications, called for advice from colleagues, tried and tried again, and finally got it right. Geraldine would be lying in the late afternoon sun right now, Freya thought, out of pain, surrounded by her family and her beloved dogs, looking out over the island she loved. She'd slip away soon, but she'd do it in peace. Thanks to Angus.

And then his head appeared around the door. He'd been doing his own paperwork next door.

'Hey,' he said. 'Busy?'

'Just finishing.' There was another thing she liked about him. He always assumed her work was just as important as his.

There were lots of things she liked about him. Maybe too many, she conceded. Like the way he was smiling right now.

Back off, she told herself and thought of how many times she'd had to say that to herself over the last three weeks. It was just that dratted smile...

'I've had a call from someone called Fred Canning,' he told her. 'It seems his wife's stuck in the bath. I could hear her yelling in the background. She says she doesn't want a lift, she wants medical help.'

Freya paused, mid filing. 'Uh-oh.'

'Uh-oh?'

'Wilma's...well, morbidly obese.'

'Really?' His smile slipped. 'So medical help...'

'Probably secondary. Unless you have a heavy-duty crane in your medical bag.'

'A job for the fire brigade?'

'I'd love to see that. Our fire brigade's all male. Wilma would have an apoplexy if they trooped into the bathroom, and the story would be all over the island by yesterday. It's a wonder she even let Fred call you.'

'Fred was expecting you to answer the clinic phone,' he said. 'That was what Wilma was yelling about. She wants the female nurse.'

'Fred's puny and has advanced arthritis. He can't lift. So I'm expected to lift her out? Me and whose army?'

'You, with me right behind you? Let's face this together.'

That made her smile. She followed him out, still smiling.

It was still with her, this wonderful feeling of being not in charge. Of sharing responsibility. Three weeks ago the idea of Wilma Canning stuck in the bath might have done her head in. Now she slid into the car beside Angus and she felt…okay.

More than okay.

This man…

She was still keeping her distance, and he respected that, but living in the same house, sharing the same garden, she couldn't help but be aware of him. And it wasn't just medical need that was changing the way she was feeling about him.

Not only did she work with him, she saw him every morning, weather permitting, playing in the garden with a recovering Seaweed. Noah had learned to throw the dog a ball. His throws were small and wild, but Seaweed reacted as if he threw them a mile. He'd race around in hysterical circles as if he couldn't find it, then finally pounce on it and drop it at Noah's feet.

How had Angus taught him to do that? He was a dog whisperer, she'd thought as she watched them.

She'd see them head to the beach in the evenings, too. From her front room she could spot them in the distance, whooping in the shallows while Seaweed tore along the beach chasing seagulls. Angus had a surfboard. He lugged it down to the beach every night, and once she'd cracked and used field glasses. She'd seen Angus lying full length on the board, with Noah lying in front of him. Every now and then a small wave would upend the board and they'd end up dunked. They'd emerge to sit in the shallows, chuckling, while Seaweed lunged gamely close—except not exactly into the water—to check what the excitement was about.

Once upon a time a child with Noah's condition could well have been placed in an institution, but now... He looked gloriously, peacefully happy. Lucky.

And Angus... She watched him laugh with his little son, unfailingly patient, unfailingly gentle, but she saw the way his eyes watched Noah and she thought Angus was lucky, too.

But every time she thought that, the pain in her gut seemed to get worse.

So put it away, she'd told herself fiercely as she'd put the field glasses away. Don't let yourself think about things that hurt. Like now. Think about Wilma Canning and the complexities of getting her out of the bath.

'Scared?' he said, glancing sideways at her, and she smiled back. This was something new, that she was relaxed enough to feel as if they could talk as friends.

Friends with reservations, though. Her barriers were there for a purpose. She'd allowed them to bend a little but there was no way they were going to break.

'I'm always scared when I go see Wilma,' she told him. 'She's one scary lady. What Wilma wants, Wilma gets.'

'She currently wants you.'

'Which is why I'm scared.'

Fred Canning was middle-aged, bald, skinny, wearing trousers that were a bit too big, held up with braces. He opened the door with the air of a man who was hunted. He didn't say a word, just walked them through the house and opened the bathroom door.

One glance and Angus could see exactly what

the problem was, but one glance was all he had before Wilma started shrieking.

Freya had been right, she was a large lady. The bath was large, but her overflowing body almost flowed right out. She had water up to her chin and it slopped on the floor. Candles were wedged onto every ledge in the room. Scented candles. An overpowering smell of gardenias poured out to greet them.

Wilma's voice was just as overpowering. 'Get out,' she ordered. 'Fred, I told you, I want Freya. A man in my bathroom... Get out!'

Angus backed out and pulled the door to almost closed. Freya went to enter but he tugged her back.

'Fred called us to help,' he told Wilma through the part-opened door, his voice as quiet as hers was loud. 'Tell us what you want us to do.'

'My toe's stuck,' she yelled. 'Idiot. Get Freya.'

He chanced another peek around the door. Yep, her toe was stuck, firmly in the tap.

'Get out!' she shrieked.

'I'm Dr Knox,' he said, through the door again. 'Angus. Have you heard of me?'

'Of course I have, but I don't want you. Tell Freya to get in here.'

'Freya's here too but we're a team.' He made his voice implacable. 'The situation you're in, you'll need more than Freya.'

'Let me go in,' Freya told him. 'I'll see if I can calm her and then you can—'

'He's not coming near me. You'll pull me out, girl,' Wilma boomed. 'I pay my taxes and that pays your wages. Just because you have some fancy doctor here, don't think you can shirk your duty. Fred can help if you need it,' she conceded. 'Not that he's been any use so far. All men are idiots.'

'She's really angry,' Fred quavered from behind them. 'I dunno how to help.'

Angus thought of the logistics. One weak male and the slight Freya. This wasn't going to work. Besides…a stuck toe. They couldn't just pull it.

'Let me go in,' Freya said again, but he put a hand on her shoulder and held her back.

'We need a plan of action,' he told her, loud enough for Wilma to hear. He didn't want Freya in there alone, subject to Wilma's bullying. 'Wilma, are you cold?'

'Yes!'

'Can you reach to let the water out?'

'If I let the water out I'll be even colder. And I can't run any warm in because my toe's stuck in the tap.'

'If you let the water out, Freya can towel you dry and then cover you with blankets.'

'Just tell her to unstick my toe.'

'Wilma, just how stuck is it?'

There was a moment's silence. Then an angry sniff. 'Very stuck,' she conceded. 'I put it in the flow so the water'd spray up like a shower. The tap must be too small. Fred ordered these taps. I should have known he'd get the wrong size.'

Fred was flattening himself against the far wall. He looked like a man who wanted, quite desperately, to run.

'So how long have you been pulling your toe?' Angus asked, quite gently, and there was another silence. Then…

'Fifteen minutes,' she said, sulkily. 'It just needs someone who can pull harder.'

He looked at Freya and saw her grimace. She'd know what they were facing. Kids did this a lot, sticking toes or fingers into taps or plug holes, experimenting with the water flow. The problem was, the more they tugged, the more swollen the toe or finger became. If she'd been pulling for fifteen minutes… Ouch.

'Carl's our fire chief,' Freya told him softly. 'He's used to cutting kids free.'

'Carl!' Wilma's voice rose in another shriek. 'If he saw me like this I'd be a laughing stock. I'd rather die.'

There was real distress now. The big lady's voice broke on a hysterical sob.

'Wilma, Freya's coming in,' he stated. They were reaching the stage where panic could be a real problem. He needed Freya to calm her down.'You're not to pull it again, though, and neither will Freya,' he told her. 'Pulling will hurt and achieve nothing. Believe me, I've been in this situation before.'

'Like I believe you,' she snapped.

'I'm a family doctor,' Angus said soothingly. 'This is what I do.' Once a kid had presented with a whole plug outlet attached to his finger.

'I won't have you in the bathroom,' she argued, past the stage of being reasonable.

'I don't need to be in there,' he told her. 'At least not until you're respectable. Freya will come in and sort you out. Fred, do you have a portable heater? That'll help.'

'But my toe,' she screeched as Fred nodded. 'I'm not having the fire brigade here. And you're still not coming in.'

'Do you have decent tools?' he asked Fred, and the little man took a deep breath, searching for courage.

'In the shed. *My* shed.' He said it almost defiantly.

'If Fred has the right gear then I can help without even coming into the bathroom,' he said to Wilma. 'Fred, can you get Freya towels, blankets and a heater. Then I want you to turn off the water at the mains and lead me to your shed.

Don't worry, Wilma, your privacy is assured. I feel a bit of plumbing coming on.'

'I'll show you the shed and get the blankets and stuff, but then… Could I make everyone a cup of tea?' Fred faltered.

'Very wise,' Angus agreed gravely. 'And if I were you, I'd take my time.'

What seemed only minutes later, Wilma was propped on cushions, covered with blankets and having trouble managing even to whinge.

That'd be due to the medication Angus had asked her to administer, Freya conceded. Based on his two swift glances he'd done an assessment of need and told her dosages. 'Just something to stop your toe throbbing,' she'd told Wilma, and the anti-anxiety and pain medication were already kicking in.

Freya had also removed the candles. 'We need your breathing to be clear,' she'd told Wilma, but in truth the smell was making her feel ill.

Coming out of the bathroom with a bucket of blown-out candles, she met Angus, loaded with tools. Doctor armed with hacksaw?

'The tap's on the outside wall,' he told her, seeing her eyes widen. 'I figure we'll cut it out, then get it off her toe when we have her free.'

'Um…you can do that?'

'I'm a man with a tool belt,' he said and grinned,

making Fred's leather tool belt swing against his thigh in a purely masculine gesture. 'Fred's shed is obviously his retreat and he has every tool you can imagine. Don't doubt me, woman.' He motioned to what she was carrying. 'I need my saw—but what's with the candles?'

'Occupational health and safety,' she said and grimaced at the smell still oozing from her armload. 'Isn't the first rule in an emergency to remove all sources of danger? These things will have me stinking of gardenias for months.'

He grinned and gave her the thumbs up, then disappeared out of the back door. Two minutes later there was the sound of banging from outside the bathroom window. Wrapped in blankets, with her leg propped on more cushions to take the weight from her toe, Wilma had started to relax. The sound roused her though, and she managed to dredge up a little more outrage. 'What the…?'

'I'm tugging off weatherboards,' Angus called through the slightly opened window. Freya would have liked to have it wide—getting rid of the gardenia smell was still a priority—but Wilma's modesty had to take precedence. 'I'm getting at your plumbing.'

'If you damage my house…'

'Isn't that what insurance is for?' he called. 'You might want to ask Fred to take a photo of you now, though, just to prove what happened.'

Wilma was rendered speechless. There was a crash from outside as one weatherboard came free—and then another.

'Where's Fred?' Wilma bleated, and Freya took her hand and held it tight. Despite the ridiculousness of her situation, to be so far out of control must be terrifying.

'He's making us all a cup of tea.' She failed to mention he'd been gone for long enough to make tea for a small army.

Coward, Freya thought, and then had to bite back a smile. If she'd had to cope alone with Wilma, she might have run, too.

Then there was the sound of an electric drill, and a moment later they saw a tiny hole appear in the wall near the tap. Wilma shrieked.

'I'm just making sure of position before I slice the inlet pipe and saw back the plaster,' Angus told her.

'You can't saw a hole in my plaster!'

'My plan is to cut the whole tap off and push it through. Then we can get you out with tap attached and remove it where we have room to work.'

'Just screw it off,' she shouted.

'You see, it's attached to you,' he said, his voice muffled but reasonable. 'And you don't…screw.'

Oh, for heaven's sake… Freya was now imagining a vision of turning a naked Wilma over and over as they unscrewed the fitting. She managed to turn a choke of laughter into a cough, but it was a close thing.

Pretend you're in Theatre, she told herself desperately. Nurse assisting surgeon.

'I'll sue…' Wilma yelled, alarm rebounding, and the sounds from outside ceased.

'You mean that?'

'If you hurt my house…'

'But we can't rescue you without it.'

'Then call someone else.'

'I'll stop now, shall I? I'll ask Fred to call the fire brigade.' There was a clatter as if tools were being gathered and Fred's head appeared the door. He looked frantic. 'Wilma…'

Freya was trying desperately not to laugh. 'Sorry…' she managed, spluttering. 'Hay fever. G-gardenias…'

'It'll be just a small hole,' Fred muttered. 'We can patch it up with something. Please let the doctor do what he has to.'

Wilma swore and swore again, and then she started noisily to weep. 'Go ahead,' she wailed through the sobs. 'Don't mind me.'

'We are minding you,' Freya said gently, pulling herself together. 'Relax, Wilma, minding you is what we're here for.'

Ten minutes later they had her out.

Once the tap was cut Freya helped her on with an oversized sweater and pants loose enough to pull on despite the attached tap. Wilma then grudgingly conceded that Angus could enter and finally they managed to get her out. By this stage she'd pretty much given up protesting. They helped her to her bedroom where she lay limp. Then Angus painstakingly cut the tap closer to the toe, leaving only a ring of metal behind. The noise of the saw was horrible, but she lay uncomplaining as Angus cut as close as he dared. He then used the age-old method of soap and string to inch the toe free.

'You'll be fine now,' Angus told her, gently massaging the bruised and swollen toe. 'There's still circulation. It'll throb a bit tonight but we'll leave you some painkillers. Isn't it lucky Fred has such a great shed? What a hero to have such tools on hand.'

Fred looked astonished, and then flashed them a look of gratification. From a useless husband he'd been elevated to a man who'd had the tools to face a crisis. They left him taking over the massaging of the toe and offering more tea—or something stronger. 'Something stronger,' Wilma moaned, and that was their signal to leave.

They made it to the car without laughing. They didn't even smirk. Who knew who might be watching from the window? They assumed rigid professional faces, doctor and nurse completing a routine house call. They pulled out of the driveway and got a hundred yards up the road before it became impossible to hold out any longer. Freya pulled her van onto the verge and buried her head in her hands.

She was laughing but silently, her shoulders heaving, her hand covering her face as she tried to suppress the almost choking chuckles.

When finally she emerged she found Angus watching her. He, too, had been chuckling but he'd stopped before she had. A smile lingered on his face but there was something else.

He was watching her as if he was seeing her for the first time. As if he was trying to make her out?

She sniffed and groped for a tissue, but he was before her, handing over a perfectly laundered handkerchief.

She subsided into it, blew her nose—and then looked at it in horror.

'I've just blown my nose on linen,' she said, astounded. 'What sort of man uses linen handkerchiefs?'

'A guy who uses disposable everything in my working life.'

'But you'll have to wash it.' For some reason she was fascinated. 'This is…you'll have to iron it too.' She tried to think of a time when she'd last ironed anything and couldn't. Wash and wear was great for work, and for gardening or the beach she used jeans, T-shirts, bathers. She had a couple of wedding and funeral outfits, but even they'd hung in the wardrobe for so long the creases had pretty much given up.

But: 'There's lots of time after Noah goes to bed,' he said and that brought her up short.

There would be, she thought. Caring for a four-year-old by himself… Lily was a childminder extraordinaire, but the Lilys of this world would be hard to find. And there'd have been trauma with the marriage split up. He'd have had to stay home with Noah.

'Come to the beach with us tonight,' he said unexpectedly into the silence.

She was still staring at the handkerchief. She thought of the two of them, Angus and Noah, heading off to the beach almost every evening, and then Noah going to sleep and Angus…ironing alone. Almost before she knew what she was doing, she found herself nodding.

What was she doing? One weak moment and she'd agreed?

But there was no going back. He was already smiling and it was a great smile. A dangerous smile.

'Friday night's our special,' he told her. 'Unless medical imperatives get in our way, we collect fish and chips at five-thirty and we're on the beach ten minutes later. In honour of your presence I'll even bring wine. If we both go, then one of us needs to limit our intake, but hopefully neither of our phones will ring. What do you say?'

'I... I'll bring a picnic rug,' she said, weakly, because she could think of nothing else to say.

'Excellent.' His smile, lingering from laughter, changed now to something warmer. It felt like a hug all by itself.

Stop it, she told herself. Cut it out with the way you're thinking. She should never have agreed to go.

'Noah will be delighted,' he told her. 'Plus Seaweed. Fish and chips on the beach...what's not to love?'

And what's to be afraid of? she demanded of herself.

Nothing at all?

CHAPTER SEVEN

FRIDAY EVENING. Fish and chips on the beach. He'd tried to do this with Noah ever since his son had started to toddle.

During their marriage Deb had deemed Friday and Saturday nights to be social. If they weren't going out or having people in, then what was wrong with them? But after Noah's birth, everything changed. Au pairs usually wanted either Friday or Saturdays off, and he hadn't been happy using casuals. In the end it was agreed that Deb would go her own way, and Friday nights would be his responsibility.

As soon as Noah was old enough they'd therefore headed to the beach, even if it meant sitting under a shelter as it rained. They'd eat fish and chips. Noah would dig or knock down the sand-castles. He'd crow with delight as they fed chips to hungry gulls, and, weather permitting, they'd paddle or swim.

Finally they'd walk home, with Noah perched

on Angus's shoulders—far preferable to Noah than being stuck in a boring pushchair—and the little boy would go to sleep content.

So they'd brought the same routine here, except it wasn't just Friday nights. This job was sometimes crazy—as it had been this afternoon—but often it wasn't. Their little 'hospital' had had three overnight patients since they'd opened—an elderly diabetic who'd needed a couple of days' monitoring, plus two patients with infections requiring intravenous antibiotics. They'd coped with them easily, so he could almost always swing dinner with Noah. Already the locals knew where 'Doc' was likely to be, and they—and Freya—had respected his need for time alone with his son.

Except tonight he wouldn't be alone.

'Freya's coming with us,' he told Noah as they collected their fishy parcel, gathered their gear and headed down the track.

'Faya…' Noah said gamely, and smiled. 'Fend.'

'She is indeed a friend.' He grinned down at his little son, happy that Noah was happy. Happy that Noah thought of 'Faya' with delight.

Noah and Freya met most mornings now, and Noah had seamlessly included her in his world. He tossed—or rather threw wildly—balls for the increasingly bouncy Seaweed, and the first time a ball had ended up near Freya he'd put his hands on his hips, fixed her with a commanding look and demanded action.

'Fow!'

She'd hesitated and then she'd thrown it, like a stranger doing a kid a favour. But Noah hadn't picked up reluctance. As far as he was concerned Freya was now part of the morning game.

So they played, and sometimes Angus had even caught her smiling. That was rare. He knew her ghosts, and he knew that a genuine smile was a gift.

To Noah?

No, to both of them.

And today things might even have changed. The shared laughter of this afternoon seemed to have broken an invisible boundary, and he was aware of irrational hope.

Could he make her smile again tonight? That was surely a quest worth pursuing.

Why?

Where did this hope spring from? The inexplicable attraction he felt for her.

Because of the way she'd dived into danger to save a drowning dog? Because of the way she smiled at Noah? She'd relaxed with Noah now, always treating him with friendly dignity.

Noah was only four and, yes, he had challenges—he'd always have challenges. Adults normally took one look at him and lowered their expectations.

'Can he speak?' Angus had lost count of the number of people who'd asked him that. And no matter how he answered, his response was often followed by: *'Oh, poor little thing.'*

Thing. It was a word he hated. Noah's speech was slow, having to force muscles other kids used involuntarily. It took him time to find and form the words he needed.

But to call him *thing.*

That last day with Deb, the words she'd flung at him, and, unforgivably, at Noah…

What was he doing, thinking of Deb and then thinking of Freya? Moving from one to the other.

Thinking of Deb's forced attempts to be kind, as opposed to the way Freya pretended to chase the ball before Seaweed pounced on one of Noah's wild throws. Thinking of how Freya could make Noah giggle.

With that thought came yet another. The memory of Freya collapsed into laughter this afternoon. And then the rest. Her background. Her tragedy.

Was he attracted to her because he felt sorry for her?

That was crazy. As a family doctor, how many appalling stories had he listened to in his lifetime?

Whatever the reason, he needed to stop, he told himself. The bottom line was that he was a single dad, caring for a child with special needs, and the last thing Freya would ever want from him was that sort of commitment.

Whoa, where were his thoughts going? Places they had no right to go, he told himself as they headed to the beach, and besides, he was getting ridiculously ahead of himself. Tonight was simply fish and chips on the beach, nothing more. She might not even turn up.

But then Noah let out an excited bellow, and he turned to see Freya coming over the sandhill. She was wearing a jonquil caftan, the soft fabric wafting around her in the gentle sea breeze. She was carrying a blanket. A bag was slung over her shoulder and he saw intriguing plastic…things… sticking out of the top.

Noah was stumbling up the sandhill, his stubby legs almost getting tangled as he hurried to meet her.

'Faya!' he crowed, and Freya dropped everything and stooped to hug him.

Seaweed joined in, jumping and barking. Freya chuckled as she fended the big dog off, turning her body to protect Noah from Seaweed's great hairy paws.

Angus's heart twisted with a jab of something so fierce, so unexpected, it left him winded.

Longing.

For a woman to hug?

No! What the hell was he thinking? He had no right.

He was mocking the direction his thoughts were taking, trying to force sense into his stupid head. He didn't need the complications of falling for his landlady and his colleague, and he suspected Freya would run a mile. Besides, he'd been on the island for a whole three weeks. How could he possibly be thinking anything of the sort?

Except he was thinking it, and somehow he had to force himself to stop.

Freya had put Noah down now. The little boy was helping her gather her belongings, then stumping back towards him with an armload of picnic rug.

'Faya,' he said proudly, and dumped the rug on top of the pile of fish and chips. Luckily still wrapped.

'I have all the toys I could find from under the house,' Freya said, plonking herself down on the sand and beaming at them both. 'And lemonade, but you did say you were bringing wine?'

He had to blink. Up until today Freya had been almost rigidly formal with him. He'd been struggling to make her smile. Now, though, it was as if she'd decided to drop all her defences at once. For this one meal? Would they go up again when the fish and chips were finished?

Take it as it comes, he advised himself as he watched Freya and Noah attack the wrapping around the fish and chips, as he listened to Freya ask Noah with all the seriousness in the world how many chips he'd like.

'Fee,' Noah announced.

Freya said, 'Me, too,' and they both proceeded to eat considerably more than three.

Take it as it comes. He did, but for the first time in a very long time—he could scarcely remember when he'd last felt like this—he found himself relaxed, grinning, arguing about who'd get the last ring of calamari, discussing the merits of lemon or vinegar, and trying to stop Noah from feeding too many chips to Seaweed.

The feeling was almost euphoric.

It had to end. He knew it did but for now…

Take it as it comes.

He was teaching his little son to surf.

Sort of.

With his belongings, Angus had brought a surfboard from the mainland and Freya knew enough about surfing to recognise a really beautiful board. It was also worn, used. Loved.

It was certainly being loved now. She was throwing balls to Seaweed while Angus was holding Noah on the board in the shallows. The little boy was lying full length—or as full length as it was possible for a four-year-old to be—waiting with almost hyper-excitement. Then he was clinging on for dear life as the small waves caught the board and carried him to the shore.

But there was no need for him to cling. Angus had him all the way, steadying the board, making sure the little boy never tumbled. And every time they reached the sand, Angus whooped with excitement, gathered him up and hugged him. They'd roll in the shallows in mutual triumph, a laughing soggy tangle, then do it all again.

It was doing something to Freya's insides. Cracking something.

Making her long for something she could never have.

In desperation she tossed the ball one last time for Seaweed, then discarded her caftan. Her swimsuit was plain, sensible. Sensible was what she needed to be, she warned herself, and headed out into deep water. She swam here often, alone, long stretches of freestyle taking her from one end of the little bay to the other.

She did that now, trying to expend energy, trying to rid herself of the way she was feeling.

She should join in their fun, she thought. She'd been invited to join them for dinner. The fish and chips had been delicious. The meal had been great.

So why couldn't she play with them now?

Because her sense was finally returning. Hard-won control, cold and firm, seemed to reform inside her as she swam. Control wasn't an enemy, it wasn't a friend, it was just part of the way she was. A survival technique. The nagging pain in her gut resurfaced as she swam, jabbing to remind her of what happened whenever she let her defences down. Emotional pain? That was what the last doctor had suggested it could be. Like ghost pain from a missing limb.

A missing baby?

Don't go there.

But emotional or not, it did hurt. Reluctantly she turned and swam to shore, just as Seaweed decided to stop chasing gulls and join Angus and Noah.

This must be the first time he'd gone into the water since they'd saved him, she thought. She'd known he'd come to the beach with them and had asked Angus about it.

'I don't think we'll ever get him swimming again,' Angus had told her. 'He thinks every wave is plotting to drown him.'

'He's a wise dog,' she'd said, but as she made her way to shore now she saw the big dog standing hock deep in the shallows, looking towards the surfers with something that appeared to be longing.

'You and me, both,' she muttered. 'But we don't belong.'

That was hardly fair. Freya's lessons had been battered into her over years, whereas Seaweed was still a pup, and it seemed one life lesson wasn't enough to protect him for ever. He made a couple of tentative dashes into the shallows and then launched himself towards Noah and Angus and the surfboard.

Noah had been lying on the board. Angus was looking behind them, watching for the next wave, but suddenly Seaweed was pouncing. He was aching to play, with no canine knowledge of what would happen if such a huge dog swamped a little boy.

But it didn't happen.

Freya surged forward just as Angus turned and grabbed, and Noah was lifted clear by both of them. Seaweed kept right on leaping. Both Freya and Angus lost their balance—still holding Noah and somehow all of them ended up tumbling in the shallows.

Safe.

Noah was between them, held out of the water. Seaweed was jumping around them, barking hysterically. Noah was squealing with delight and Angus hugged him tight and laughed.

'Well done us. Another great save, Nurse Freya.'

'My splinter skill,' she managed. 'Lifesaver.'

'Um…lifesaver? We didn't quite qualify as being in mortal peril.'

Then they couldn't speak because Seaweed gave an almighty shake. Water flew everywhere and Noah shrieked with laughter.

And Freya thought, what a kid. How many four-year-olds would react to what had just happened with instinctive laughter?

Only ones with total trust that they were loved, she thought. Only those who knew absolutely that their dad would never let them be hurt.

This man…

Angus.

They were still far too close, with Noah between them. Angus's shoulder was brushing hers.

She felt…she felt…

'How about a surf yourself?' she said, hurriedly, because suddenly she needed a way to break this intimacy, this feeling that was doing her head in.

'Sorry?' Angus was still chuckling, holding Noah close to protect him from the worst of the spray. Seaweed had obviously decided that this was a great game. He was crouching in the shallows, barking, then leaping to his feet and shaking, over and over.

It was like being in a constant shower, with the

warmth of the evening and the benign temperature of the sea making it okay.

More than okay, Freya thought. More than fun, too. What was forming between this little group contained more than a trace of something she'd once longed for.

Something she knew she couldn't have.

'I've had a decent swim,' she managed, desperate to break what she didn't understand. What she was most afraid of. 'You…you haven't. In fact…' She hesitated, looking at his obviously well-used surfboard. 'Have you even surfed since you came to the island?'

'Noah and I surf most nights.'

'But by yourself?'

'It's fine,' Angus said, a bit stiffly. 'We have fun, don't we, Noah?'

'I'm sure you do, but I'm betting you've not only stayed in the shallows, you've also stayed within hearing of your phone. But I can stay within earshot of your phone now, and there are some great waves far out. Noah, did you know I have grapes in my bag? Would you like to eat grapes and make sandcastles while your daddy goes into the big waves and shows us how to stand up on his surfboard?'

'Gapes,' Noah said, gamely trying to follow the conversation. And then as he sorted out important words from unimportant, he struggled out of Angus's arms and looked up at the beach.

'Gapes,' he said again, and the thing was decided.

'You're sure this is okay?' Angus said, but she could hear the longing in his voice. She knew instinctively that this was a man with surfing in his blood. In truth it wasn't only instinct. It was the condition of his board—plus she'd noticed a faded, tell-tale scar running almost from knee to ankle. She'd seen this type of scar before, mostly on young men, mostly caused by novice surfers cutting in on each other. How many surfers' legs had she stitched in her time back on the island? She'd lost count, and it was always a challenge keeping them out of the water long enough for their cuts to heal. Surfing was addictive.

Angus had been on the island for almost a month, and in all that time he'd only been in the shallows.

'Go,' she said gently. 'If I need you or if we get a call I'll wave you in, but hopefully it's too good a night for any self-respecting islander to have a medical emergency. If Noah gets tired I'll wrap him up in towels and tell him a story. Surf as long as you want. We'll be happy.'

At which he cast her a searching look—one that said he didn't quite believe the happy bit. That said she'd told him too much already and he was probably guessing the rest.

But then he looked at his surfboard and she could see it was like a siren's song.

'Go,' she urged—and he went.

CHAPTER EIGHT

THE SURF WAS GREAT. More than great, it was fantastic, but he wasn't going to push it. He surfed for twenty minutes, caught three magnificent waves, rode the last one to shore and pulled his board out of the water.

Noah and Freya strolled down to meet him. Seaweed too, though he came slower because he was dragging an enormous lump of kelp. He was wagging his tail as if he'd just found forty-seven bones.

Noah was holding Freya's hand, trustfully. Happily.

They all looked happy.

'Did you want to come out, or are you thinking you should come out?' Freya asked, and he had to be honest.

'It's great out there,' he confessed, and he turned to look back at the ocean and he couldn't quite keep regret from his voice.

'And it's great here, too,' she said, smiling. They were on daylight saving time. Dusk hadn't even started to fall, and the beach was lovely. 'Noah and I have been thinking we might build a fire. We thought we'd walk up to the house and get some matches—plus there's a bag of marshmallows in my pantry I happen to have stashed for just such an occasion. We thought we'd gather driftwood and light ourselves a beach fire. I'm betting they don't let you light beach fires on your Sydney beaches.'

'No,' he said faintly. 'They don't.'

'Then is it okay with you if we do?'

'I…maybe…it's Noah's bedtime.'

'No,' Noah said, very definite.

'If Daddy says it's bedtime, then I can take you home and read you a story there,' she told him. And then she looked back to Angus. 'But alternatively, we could bring an extra blanket down in case we get tired after marshmallows. You could then surf all you want and keep an eye on us as well.'

What an offer! To surf all he wanted. More, to surf while Noah was safe on the beach, in sight, happy… He glanced at Noah, who was looking up at him with hopeful eyes. Seaweed had dropped his kelp and he looked expectant as well.

And Freya? She'd made the offer cautiously, he thought, and he wasn't sure whether the caution was because she was worried about his reaction—or worried that she was overstepping her own boundaries. The latter, he thought, with sudden perception, and he knew his answer had to be yes.

So he gave his gracious permission and tried not to feel like an excited schoolkid who'd been given an unexpected holiday. He stooped and hugged Noah and had to consciously make a decision not to hug Freya as well.

He didn't. He wasn't an idiot, but it was an effort not to. Then he turned and headed back into the waves and it was glorious.

This beach, down from Freya's house, was almost always deserted, and the surf here was one of the reasons he'd thought of coming to Shearwater. It was even better than he'd imagined. Apart from scores of tiny sandpipers scurrying up and down the beach, they had the place to themselves.

The waves were picture-perfect, cresting magnificently to gorgeous curves, breaking in long, low runs across the breadth of the bay. The green room—formed when the waves wrapped surfers in walls of transparent sapphire and white— seemed to happen every third or fourth wave. Magic.

How could he not surf on, transported to a place he'd just about forgotten?

How could he not feel he'd been teleported to a time when he was free of a city he'd started to loathe, of the heartbreak that had been his marriage, of the sometimes overwhelming responsibility of loving his little son on his own?

He'd never shelve that responsibility—he'd never want to—but for this night it had somehow been lifted from him. Not by a paid babysitter, but by a friend, and a friend who was obviously enjoying herself. From time to time he glanced back at the beach and he saw happiness. He saw a fire being made, flickering to life. He saw woman and child and dog trawling the beach for more driftwood. He saw them settle to the serious business of toasting marshmallows.

As his waves took him near the shore he saw Noah settle, covered with a blanket, his head on Freya's lap. Was she telling him stories? Was she singing to him? Or was that all part of the fantasy of this night?

There was an urge to go listen as well, but he knew instinctively that the stories would stop as soon as he got there. The defences would go up again.

When the longest of the waves drove him all the way in, he stood in the shallows and looked questioningly at the little group, but Freya waved him back away.

'We're happy,' she called. 'Surf as long as you want.'

Was she happy? Probably not, he thought, but

it was too great a night to question, and when the sun finally sank in a great tangerine ball, casting a golden glow over the ocean, he hauled his board up the beach feeling more at peace than he had for years.

She was watching him come, sitting beside the fire, the flames flickering across her face in the fading light. Noah was snuggled in a blanket, his head still on her lap, sound asleep. She'd been wearing a plain black swimsuit, simple, almost severe. Before that she'd worn the floaty sarong, but now she'd tossed on a towelling beach robe, soft green, warm.

She looked up at him as he approached and smiled, and that smile did something to his insides. Something tangled, ill-defined, but as warm as the two of them looked.

Seaweed was crouched on the other side of the fire, snoozing his contentment with this new order of his life. He looked up and wagged his tail as Angus grew near.

That was pretty much how Angus was feeling.

He dumped his board and snagged a towel, busying himself with vigorous drying. His thoughts were flying in all sorts of directions. He needed to get his head in order.

'I thought you might stay out there for the night, you looked so happy,' Freya told him. 'You're a great surfer.'

'Once upon a time I planned to be a professional surfer,' he admitted. 'I decided when I was eight. I'd get myself a board, head off round the world and surf every single wave I could find.'

'Why didn't you?'

'Life decisions made when you're eight don't normally factor in practicalities,' he told her, shoving away a momentary memory of his parents' intransigence. Law or medicine or nothing. 'What did you want when you were eight?'

'Pretty much what I have now,' she said. Noah stirred in his sleep, and she gently removed him from her lap, settling him by her side, pillowed on a heap of towels. 'A garden, a beach, a...' She stopped and bit her lip. 'Well, not much more, really.'

'You were going to say a family, weren't you?'

What the...? *Why the hell had he asked that?* It was just about the most intrusive question he could have asked, and he got exactly what he deserved. He saw a wash of pain cross her face that was so deep, so powerful that he stooped before he could stop himself and put his hands on her shoulders.

'Hell. Freya, I'm so sorry. I should never have said it.'

''S okay.'

But it wasn't. He heard the muffled anguish in her terse reply. He knelt so he was looking at her. His hands tightened on her shoulders and he waited. Her head was bowed but finally she looked up at him.

Faces, six inches apart. Pain in waves.

'I have…there's potatoes in the ashes. We buried them,' she managed.

'Freya, I am so sorry,' he said again, his gaze not leaving hers. 'After what you've told me of your past, that was the cruellest thing I could have said.'

'But the truth.'

She closed her eyes for a minute and he saw her fight for control. When she opened them again she almost had it.

'I guess… Mum was always ill and Grandma was busy. Mum's medications cost us a heap. The rest of the family helped out as well—Uncle Gary, others—but Mum had to go back and forth to Sydney for treatment so Grandma worked her butt off, doing other people's housework. When she was home she'd garden, sometimes I think almost obsessively as she saw Mum get worse. I used to help her and I loved it, but sometimes, when I saw other kids on the beach with their families, I dreamed… Well, that was that, just a kid's dream. No drama, Angus.'

It was a drama though, he thought. When she'd been about to say family, he knew it wasn't the loss of her childhood family she was thinking of. It was a tiny baby girl…

'Have a potato,' she said, hurriedly, roughly turning the subject. 'We buried them in the ashes ages ago and I bet you're hungry.'

He was. It was a solid thing he could do, to scrape cooked potatoes from the ashes, load them with the butter and cheese she'd brought back from the house, eat them slowly—wow, they were hot—and wait for the world to settle. Wait for her to settle.

'Coffee?' she asked, producing a thermos and that took time, too. It didn't matter. Blessedly the phone didn't ring. Noah and Seaweed were deeply asleep. There seemed all the time in the world.

She needed that time, he thought, and so did he. He needed space for his hurtful words to subside, for the peace of this night to do its own healing. He sat and drank coffee and watched the moon rise, and the silence between them slowly, imperceptibly changed to something else.

A waiting.

'We…we should head home,' Freya said at last. 'Noah needs his bed.'

'Noah's happier right now than he's ever been,' he murmured. 'For that matter, so am I.' He turned and took her empty mug from her hands, putting it on the sand, setting his own down carefully beside it. As if it were vitally important that the mugs were lined up together. He stared down at them for a long moment and then looked up at Freya.

She looked calmly back. Something had happened in these last few minutes, he thought. Something had changed.

'Freya,' he said, softly into the silence. He took her hands and held them, firmly, surely. 'I hurt you tonight with my words. I would never consciously hurt you. I swear.'

'I know that.' But her voice shook a little and he thought, no, she doesn't know it.

'Your toerag husband… He's not a standard of the male species. You were so damned unlucky.'

'I was.'

'You've had no relationships since?'

'I wouldn't want one.'

'Really?' He hesitated. 'Are you sure? Because, Freya, I'd really, really like to kiss you right now. But I won't do it unless you want it too. I'll never do anything you don't want.'

'I…'

'Is there any reason you wouldn't want me to kiss you?'

Silence. A long silence. She was looking into his face, the flickering firelight showing him the cascade of emotions flooding across hers.

Doubt. Fear. Longing.

But in the end the longing won. He saw the

moment her face changed, softened. He saw the fear disappear—or maybe not disappear but be put away, shelved for now, told to wait and see.

'Yes?' he said, smiling into her eyes, and her eyes were suddenly smiling back.

'Yes,' she breathed and then there was no room for any other words at all.

What was she doing? How had this happened? Why was she letting it…?

And that was where her thoughts stopped, right there. As his mouth descended on hers she felt panic like a lightning strike—and then they were kissing and the panic simply evaporated. Gone. Forgotten.

There was only Angus.

If she still had her faculties, she'd remember that she'd made a vow never to let anyone close. Never to let anyone pierce the shell of self-protection she'd so carefully built around herself. She'd had no intention of kissing anyone.

She'd certainly had no intention of kissing Angus. He was her colleague. He was her tenant. Kissing such a man would only lead to complication upon complication upon complication.

But this kiss had no intention behind it, nor did it have regard to consequences. It was an instinctive, almost primeval response to a longing she hadn't known until this moment that she was capable of. She'd agreed to be kissed before her defences caught up with desire.

Desire was demanding she be kissed, and it was demanding that she kiss him right back.

Even then, surely the kiss should have been tentative, the first gentle exploration of something that seemed to be growing between them. But there was nothing tentative about this kiss. Or about the way she was feeling. Yes, there should have been, but *should* didn't seem to be happening. *Would* had taken over. She *would* kiss him, sensible or not.

Forces bigger than both of them were in play here.

His hands had caught her face. His lovely, long fingers were cradling her cheeks as he kissed her, and the feel of him… The taste, the smell, the strength… The need…

It felt like…a kiss to change her world?

That was a stupid thing to think, but then there was no room for thought.

There was only this man.

And as his hands held her close, as tenderness and care and mutual longing engulfed her, things changed.

She was a woman who'd spent years building a shell of self-protection. She'd learned what happened if she let down her defences, and she carried her grief for her baby like a shield.

And Angus—who was he? He was a man who seemed to have been in a loveless marriage. He'd walked away to protect his child, but who knew anything about him apart from that?

Did he want another family?

Family… Angus's mention of the word should have warnings flashing like neon lights right now, but there was no space for thoughts inside her head, not in this cocoon of firelight, of warmth, of want, of need.

Not in the touch of her mouth meeting his. Not in the way his hands held her face, drew her into him, deepening the kiss.

Not in the way her body responded.

Oh, she needed this. It was a need that was beyond reason, and if he'd drawn back now she would have fought him every inch of the way.

His kiss was deepening still further. His hold was stronger, surer, and her hands went around his body and held him in their turn. Oh, the feel of him…

The beach, the night, the sleeping child, the snoozing dog, they'd all faded. There was only this man. The bleakness of the past had some-how disappeared. For this moment there was only Angus, and the feel of his body, and his hands drawing her close.

Closer.

'Freya…' His voice was a ragged whisper, and

she could hear the desire in it. The raw need. 'We can't…'

Of course, they couldn't. They might want to—and she wanted to very much—but some vestige of sense remained. They were on a beach in the firelight, and the beach, though isolated, was still public. Fishermen came along here at night.

Noah was sleeping beside them. Seaweed, too. The phone might ring.

Somehow common sense had to prevail.

'I guess…we can't.'

'Rendezvous back at the house?' There was a trace of laughter in his voice, tenderness, a smile.

But the break had let rationality edge back in, giving her space to grab for caution.

'I… No. Angus, it's too…'

'Soon,' he finished for her, and smiled again, that lovely, caring smile that melted her insides and then some. 'I agree. Too soon. How about tomorrow?'

She found herself smiling back. Tomorrow? Or maybe the next day? For the first time in years she felt herself tingle with anticipation. When she walked out into the garden at breakfast time, he'd be there. Angus. With his son. With his dog.

Family.

And for the first time, the word didn't make her cringe. It must be the night, she thought. Or there was something in the coffee. Some hallucinogenic substance that was making her forget all the hard lessons she'd learned.

But still she found she was continuing to smile, and when he reached for her again she sank into a second kiss. It was shorter than the first but somehow sweeter, because it felt like a promise of things to come.

'Maybe tomorrow,' she whispered as finally they broke apart. 'Or...or the day after.'

'Or the day after that,' he told her and put his finger on her lips, as if placing a seal there. 'No rush, my lovely Freya. We have all the time in the world.'

CHAPTER NINE

THE MORNING BROUGHT SENSE—sort of. She woke and the sun was streaming in her open windows. Noah was giggling out on the front lawn and Seaweed was barking…and for a moment she lay and let herself bask in a half-asleep dream of what life could have been.

Maybe still could be? In this dreamy state it even seemed possible that she could take this further.

That *they* could take things further. A divorced man and woman. Why not?

And then one of her customary tummy twinges hit. She winced and clenched on the pain, letting it ride itself out, and thought it was like a stern teacher, reminding her to behave. Reminding her of consequences.

'Stuff you,' she said out loud, but the lesson had been learned. She knew she had to be sensible.

Still, the morning was indeed gorgeous, and

she didn't have clinic for another couple of hours. If she didn't make herself coffee and toast and join them, they'd think something was wrong.

Nothing was wrong. She was a woman in control.

A woman who'd been kissed.

But a woman who was moving on, a mature woman to whom one…okay, two…sweet kisses weren't life-changing. She showered and dressed—for some reason it seemed important that this morning she didn't stroll out there in her pyjamas. She made herself coffee and toast and took herself outside.

They were out by her rose bush. Scent from Heaven.

'Faya!' Noah yelled as he saw her, and the happiness in his voice made a lump form in her throat. She hadn't realised how much this little boy was wriggling his way into her heart. As she came close, he lobbed Seaweed's ball wildly towards her, and for once it reached her. Shocked, she dropped her coffee and caught the ball. Her mug didn't break, but there went her coffee. Her toast slid sideways and Seaweed pounced, but Noah was beaming at her as if all his Christmases had come at once.

So who cared about coffee and toast? 'Faya!' he shouted, triumphant. 'Faya caught ball.'

Wow. Noah's tosses were so wild she defied

anyone to try and catch one, but that wasn't the important thing right now. For most kids with Down's syndrome, articular accuracy was a huge challenge, a massive struggle to make muscles coordinate. That he'd managed a three-word sentence... Yes!

She glanced across and Angus's smile was as wide as hers.

'Hooray,' he said, strolling across to greet her. He looked down at the remains of her coffee, and then across to Seaweed, bolting to the far side of the garden with his prize. 'Pity about breakfast.'

'What's more important?' she managed. 'Coffee and toast, or catching one soggy ball?'

'Or saying one three-word sentence.' Before she could guess what he intended, he removed the ball from her hand, tossed it back to Noah, then leaned forward and kissed her. On the lips. Lightly. It was a kiss of good morning. It was a kiss of...

Lovers?

Something was shifting inside her. Something important.

And then there was another whoop as Noah tossed the ball again. His aim was getting better and so was his strength. The ball rose high above their heads, falling to earth in a small patch of violets, planted in the dappled shade to the side of her lovely rose.

'Daddy!' Noah shouted imperatively, and Angus grinned and went to retrieve it.

And then he stopped.

The violets had been planted meticulously, and with love. The flowers looked almost innocuous—an extension of ground cover—unless you looked with care.

They formed a scattering of sweet-smelling mauve blooms among a backdrop of deep green leaves. Tucked into the centre was a tiny patch of white violets, in the shape of a heart.

Angus stared down for a long moment, his face impassive. Then he retrieved the ball and carefully brushed the crushed flowers so they stood upright again. He looked up at her, his eyes infinitely gentle. 'Chloe,' he said softly, and she managed to nod.

'I'm so sorry,' he said softly. 'I won't let it happen again. They're not damaged. I won't let Noah…'

'Don't you dare stop him playing here,' she said, almost fiercely. 'Chloe would have… Noah and Chloe…it's okay.'

He got it. Somehow she knew he understood how desperate she was that Chloe could stay, in some tiny way, a part of her life, and if that meant Noah's ball landed on her grave, then that was okay with her.

More than okay.

He rose and came to her, brushing her face with his fingers. A breath of a caress. 'You're wonderful,' he told her. 'You and your daughter.'

'Don't. Angus, I...' She backed off a little, fighting to recall her sanity. 'Sorry, I...'

'You need more toast and coffee. I can see that.' His smile was a kiss all by itself, and she knew he realised there were emotions threatening to overwhelm her. 'Shall we go inside and make some?'

'I can't.' She sounded panicked.

'Then don't,' he told her, still smiling that smile that did her head in. 'Sorry, Freya, that was a liberty, but, dammit, this place shouldn't be so lovely, and your daughter's grave shouldn't be so perfect. You shouldn't be so perfect. However, it won't happen again. I told you last night, there's no rush. Or I'll back off completely if that's what you want.' His eyes were serious, steady. *What I say is true.*

Her world settled a little. Panic subsided, but it didn't completely go away. The touch of his mouth on hers...the steadfastness of his gaze... the sheer kindness of the man...

'I didn't need breakfast anyway,' she managed, and he took her plate from her hand and stooped and retrieved the coffee mug.

'You do, you know,' he said gently. 'But Noah and I have had ours, and my kettle's still hot. How about you two see if you can repeat the catching miracle while I make you a refill?'

'I can...'

'Make toast instead of miracles?' He smiled. 'I'm sure you can, but with Noah... It takes a special kind of woman to do what you're doing. Leave me the plebeian tasks, Ms Mayberry, and see if another miracle is just around the corner.' His smile softened, aimed straight at her, straight at her heart? 'Miracles are worth working for, don't you think?'

Hmmph. And double *hmmph.*

It was all very well for Angus to talk of miracles, but there was no such thing. She knew it, and if he didn't know it too then he ought. Watching a little boy learn to talk was one thing. Beach campfires and surfing and unwise kisses were another entirely.

She needed to mind her own business, she told herself as the morning progressed. Her business was keeping the islanders healthy and maintaining her grandmother's garden.

The problem was, these things had once taken up a hundred per cent of her time, and now Angus was here they didn't. And even more importantly, they didn't keep her away from Angus.

That morning she was running a learning group for expectant mums in the hall, but at the same time Angus was seeing patients in the nearby clinic. When her group broke for morning tea, Angus wandered in as he'd taken to doing. He snagged a mug of tea and a lamington—no islander gathering ever happened without snacks—and mixed easily with her soon-to-be mums.

It worked a treat. By now he'd done it so often, her mums were relaxing with him, so much that she knew if there was any problem during labour they'd be prepared to trust his advice, trust him. But as good as it was, it meant pressure. On her.

But it was a covert pressure, maybe one he didn't even know he was exerting. He'd move among her mums, seemingly totally at ease, drawing each of them out, getting to know them…and it wasn't a superficial interest either. His interest was real and personal, and the islanders, usually slow to open up to strangers, were reacting to him in a way that seemed to make the pressure inside her even worse.

But was worse the wrong word? Yes, because pressure that was unwanted had to be bad. She didn't want to feel the way she was feeling.

That afternoon there was no medical need, something that had seldom happened when Angus wasn't here, but was now increasingly common. Noah napped in the afternoon and Lily had started taking him to her place, 'So I can have a wee nap myself.' Freya was thus free to garden, to dig in the loamy soil, to prepare her beds for the next round of home-grown vegetables.

The garden was her place of peace, but even here, an hour after she'd started, Angus joined her.

The first time he'd offered to help, she should have told him no, but that would have seemed surly. He'd offered to tackle the great clumps of agapanthus her grandmother had unwisely put in years ago. They were now threatening to take over the world, so she'd grudgingly said yes, and then managed to produce a small smile. So this afternoon here he was again. He worked at the other end of the garden, but still he was…here.

He wasn't a chatterer. He clearly respected her peace. He even seemed to realise what a joy this was, to work steadily to make this beautiful place even more beautiful.

So they worked apart. They could almost be strangers and yet the feeling she had…he most definitely wasn't a stranger.

Occasionally she couldn't resist glancing at him, and sometimes he caught her doing the same. When that happened he'd smile, but keep on doing what he was doing. He was attacking the agapanthus with hoe and shovel, stripped to the waist, his bare back glistening with sweat. He was heaving debris across to the compost bins.

He was swearing when the phone rang in his pocket and he knew he'd have to turn back into a doctor again.

Those calls often meant that he needed to leave, and Freya should be grateful—if they didn't require her to accompany him, she'd have her garden back to herself again. But always as he left she was aware of a stab of loss, and that added to her confusion as well.

Stop it, she told herself, over and over, but there was no way she could define '*it*'.

Or maybe there was.

Maybe, a tiny voice was starting to whisper in her head. Maybe, maybe, maybe.

Don't go there.

She just had to put her head down and keep going. She had to keep reminding herself what was at stake.

Gardens were safe. Medicine was safe. Angus Knox was most definitely not safe at all.

Saturday morning, two months to the day since Angus had arrived on the island, Marc rang and quizzed him about his long-term intentions. The agreement had been for a two-month trial and then a decision on the future. It was now time for that decision.

Angus had just returned from a house call on the far side of the island. An old fisherman was nearing the end of a long illness. He was barely conscious but comfortable and with no pain, slipping out of this world with peace. He was sleeping by his favourite window, overlooking the sea, surrounded by kids and grandkids, and Angus had driven home thinking this was about as far from the practice he'd had in Sydney as it was possible to get.

How good was this island? And his life here. His medical practice was sometimes a bit too exciting, but seldom overloaded. He had plenty of time for Noah.

And for Freya.

Speaking of what was happening with Freya… The more he saw of her, the more he thought… maybe.

'As long as the islanders are happy, as long as Freya's happy, then you can regard me as permanent,' he told Marc.

'Then you're definitely permanent,' Marc said firmly. 'We've heard nothing but good about you from the islanders. We've talked to Freya, too, and she's impressed with your competence.'

Impressed with his competence? It seemed a bland compliment, but he'd take it.

'I imagine you'll want your own place to live,' Marc told him, moving on. 'We have a team of builders working here on Gannet, plus an architect who's spending a week here every month. You want me to ask them to get in touch?'

'I... Not yet.'

'Yeah, the islanders say you seem pretty happy staying with Freya.' Marc chuckled. 'Good luck with that.'

'Marc...'

And then the smile died from Marc's voice. 'Mate, a warning. You know my wife—Elsa? She's lived on these islands most of her life—the same as Freya. She says if you mess with Freya, you mess with her. Elsa and Freya are both island women and...well, that they're not to be messed with is putting it mildly. Got it?'

'I have it,' Angus acknowledged.

'Just so you know,' Marc said. 'But that aside... welcome to permanence, Dr Knox. Here's to happy ever after.'

Happy ever after.

It had a good ring to it. A solid ring.

Saturday morning there was no clinic, and Freya had offered to take care of Noah while he did the house call. Marc had rung just as he'd arrived home.

He looked out at the garden now. Freya and Seaweed and Noah were planting bulbs. Or sort of planting. Freya was digging holes, popping bulbs in and covering them up. Noah was watering, turning the bed into a mud bath. Seaweed was coming behind digging them all up again.

No one seemed to mind. He knew Freya would replant her bulbs while the two of them had their afternoon sleeps. She had infinite patience.

A woman not to be messed with.

He had no intention of…messing…with her, but the more he saw of her, the more the feeling grew that here was someone of infinite worth. These last few weeks of waiting for her defences to crack had started to feel endless.

There were qualms—of course there were qualms. If things didn't turn out between them…

He walked out to the garden and stood watching them. Freya and Noah. A small boy he loved with all his heart.

A woman he suspected he was starting to love in equal measure.

Despite the pleasure of the phone call, a tiny flag of self-preservation was waving internally, and waving hard. He'd had one failed marriage and he'd been lucky to save Noah from the life-long heartache that could have resulted from that. If things didn't work out with Freya, if he let himself go down the road his heart was ordering him to follow, it might mean more than just him got hurt.

But then Freya looked up and saw him and she smiled, and how could he help but smile back at her? How could he possibly not take the road his heart was dictating?

'What?' she said. 'You look like the cat that got the cream.'

'I've just been offered a job,' he told her, and her smile died. Was he imagining it, or did she actually blanch? That'd be wishful thinking, he told himself, and strolled down to meet her.

She was filthy. She had gardening gloves on but, with the mud Noah and his hose were producing, wrist-length gloves were worse than useless. Her shorts and T-shirt were splattered with mud, and her bare legs above her wellingtons were nearly black. A streak of soil was smeared from ear to nose, and at some stage she must have run her gloved fingers through her short-cropped hair.

There were freckles on the end of her nose.

She looked worried.

She looked gorgeous.

He had an almost irresistible urge to kiss her. He didn't—somehow he'd managed to hold himself back over the last few weeks. Instead he took her by the waist and spun her round in a silly, exuberant twirl. He smiled into her worried face and then set her down, fiercely fighting that urge to kiss her.

To claim her.

'It's a good job, then?' she managed, and he could hear she was fighting to stay calm.

'A great job. Something to celebrate with a spin. Or two.' For good measure he picked up Noah and spun him, too, hose and all. The water hit Seaweed, who yelped and bolted to a safe distance, where he proceeded to bark his indignation.

Freya had herself under control now—or almost. She attempted to swipe the mud from her face and only succeeded in adding more. 'A job,' she managed. 'Back…back in Sydney?'

'Here,' he told her because, much as he'd loved seeing that lurch of dismay, the last thing he wanted was to worry this woman.

This woman. Freya.

'That was Marc from Gannet Island,' he told her. 'You know I'm on two months' probation? Marc's just rung to say my Shearwater colleague—that would be you—has given me a pretty good rap. Thank you very much, Nurse Mayberry. The islanders seem satisfied with my service as well, so on the basis of their recommendations Marc's offered to make my contract permanent. And I said yes.'

'Oh, Angus…'

'Another spin?' he asked, and she looked up into his face and she chuckled and she said:

'Definitely another spin.'

So he did, while Noah and Seaweed bounced with excitement. Then, as the spin came to an end, Angus could resist no longer. He had her in his arms, she was looking up at him, smiling her beautiful smile, and he'd have to be inhuman not to kiss her.

So he kissed her and it seemed his world righted itself, right there and then.

'Kiss,' Noah said and wiggled his way between them. Seaweed squeezed in as well, and suddenly they were ensconced in a group hug that felt… fantastic.

And when Seaweed got a trifle too exuberant and they were forced to pull away, Freya's eyes were shining. With tears? Maybe, but there was no sadness. This was okay.

Don't mess with her. Marc's message had been a warning but how could he ever dream of messing with her?

'Lunch,' he said, because he had to say something—and something prosaic seemed the safest option right now. What he really wanted to say was far deeper, far stronger, but he'd known Freya for two months now and he knew the fear of trusting was always there. It might take him a lifetime to banish it completely, he thought, but, hey, suddenly such a lifetime project seemed the most desirable thing in the world.

He'd take his time. He'd accepted permanence

as a doctor. Permanence in Freya's life was something he wanted even more.

'Lunch,' she responded, a trifle unsteadily. 'I… I have a salad inside, and fresh bread. You want to come in and share?'

This was a step forward all by itself. In the whole time he'd been there he'd never been invited 'next door'. Noah had taken to popping in and out of Freya's side of the house—by invitation—but no such invitation had ever been issued to Angus. The beach and the garden were common ground, but her side of the house was just that. Hers.

He went to accept—and then he hesitated. Despite the spins, the kiss, the heady excitement, there was still that wariness in her eyes. That cloud that said she was afraid of moving too fast.

He wouldn't do it. He wouldn't push. Her boundaries had to be her boundaries, and she had to be sure. When…if…she wanted him, it had to be her call.

But still he wanted a celebration. A real celebration.

This seemed too big an occasion to mark with a salad.

It was almost midday and the day was gorgeous. Noah was leaning against his legs, deeply content but more than ready for lunch and a nap. Seaweed, too, needed a rest.

There was bookwork to be done—his medico-legal work was catching up with him. Freya probably wanted to continue gardening without her 'helpers'. He should have a quick lunch, then settle to a separate afternoon.

He didn't want to.

'What if I check if Lily's free?' he found himself suggesting. 'Could I ring Blue Water Resort and find out if they have any reservations available? If Lily can take care of Noah, we could have a proper celebratory meal?'

She didn't exactly freeze. She didn't seize it with both hands, either.

'A date, you mean?'

The wariness had slammed back. 'A date,' he said, cautiously. 'The very hint of which has you running a mile?'

'No, I…' She managed a self-deprecating smile. 'That was dumb.'

'Not dumb,' he told her. 'Practical. Setting the ground rules makes sense. Like booking for a short medical appointment when you know you have a list a mile long, it's kinder for all parties to be honest. So not a date. A one-course meal and a glass of soda water on the side? Whatever makes you comfortable.'

She flushed. 'Sorry. It's just that I like…'

'To know where you stand.' He softened, looking at the doubt. The fear. 'Freya, it's not a "date" as such.' Even though he'd like it to be. 'It should be a mutual celebration—the satisfaction of colleagues who've sorted themselves the medical set-up of their dreams.'

'It is…a great outcome.'

'It certainly is. So…if Lily's available, if there's room for us at the restaurant, will you come?'

'Yes,' she said, and smiled, and he could see the fear had suddenly disappeared.

He wanted to whoop. He wanted—quite badly—to pick her up and spin again.

Instead he picked up Noah and whistled to Seaweed.

'Excellent,' he told her, managing to keep his tone prosaic. 'I'll call the resort and let you know the outcome.'

'Thank you,' she said, quite formally. One colleague to another. 'I'll go and clean up. For my formal celebration with my colleague.'

CHAPTER TEN

IT WAS A DATE.

No, it was a celebratory lunch between colleagues.

She was trying to decide what to wear.

Oh, for heaven's sake, she'd been working with the man for two months. He was a doctor, she was a nurse and they'd just decided to make their work partnership permanent.

He'd spun her and he'd kissed her.

More than that, though, he'd become her friend. He lived in the back half of her place. His kid and his dog played in her garden, played with her. He helped with the heavy work—he'd rid the place of every clump of agapanthus.

Their coming had eased her isolation.

It had inched through a few barriers.

Friendship was an insidious thing, she decided, staring at a crimson dress she'd had in her wardrobe for years and hadn't touched except for the island Christmas party. But she decided on a pair of white trousers and a soft apricot blouse instead. Yes, this was a celebration, but she didn't want him to get any ideas.

Except…he already had those ideas. She could see it in the way he looked at her. There was a kind of hunger in his eyes.

Which matched hers.

'Don't be stupid,' she told her reflection as she brushed her curls and tried to find the mascara wand she hadn't used since…well, since the last Christmas party, probably.

But she was being stupid. Or something else. She felt…happy.

Because Angus was staying, and she wanted him to stay? This island was a whole lot safer with a doctor here, and he was a great doctor. Skilled, empathic, kind…

Sexy as hell.

She glanced down at the red dress with a kind of longing.

'Just colleagues,' she told herself severely, and she headed out of the door in her sensible trousers and blouse.

But…just colleagues?

She didn't believe it one bit.

Blue Water Resort was at the far end of the island, on a headland where it seemed as though you could look almost all the way to Hawaii. The restaurant was as far out on the headland as it was possible to build.

This place deserved worldwide acclaim, Angus thought. All they could see as they approached was a semi-circle of stone and glass—and that view. He'd never been here until now and it took his breath away.

'Stunning, hey?' Freya said at his side and he had to resist an almost irresistible urge to take her hand. To walk into this place as a couple.

He knew without trying that such an act would have her pulling away.

He knew without asking what a huge step coming out to this lunch with him had been.

The phone in his pocket was silent. Please let it stay that way, he demanded of the universe. One or both of them was always on call. One trivial incident could mess with this.

He remembered Deb's fury whenever he was called away during a meal. Freya wouldn't be angry, he thought. But maybe she'd be disappointed.

Or gutted. The way he was feeling it'd be him who'd feel gutted.

And then he was distracted. A massive Moreton Bay fig, one of the biggest trees he knew, overshadowed the entrance. A wide bench had been built beside it, and on it was a man, midforties, sitting alone in the shade.

'Hi, Robbie.' Freya greeted him with easy charm.

Angus recognised him, too. Robbie Veitch.

He'd seen Robbie around the town from time to time, often in tow with his elderly mother. Like Noah, the big man had Down's syndrome. Unlike Noah, he didn't speak. When Angus saw him he was usually shambling along beside Betty, carrying her basket, silent but seemingly amiable.

He'd been watching them come, and as Freya greeted him, he smiled and waved, as if he recognised her. He was holding a hefty sandwich in the hand he was waving. A single red balloon was attached to the bench beside him. He looked content, but to Angus's shock he saw a cord attached from his belt to the wooden bench.

'What the hell...?' he demanded, but Freya was smiling.

'How's it going, Robbie?'

The big man beamed and waved some more, seemingly happy. He had a bottle of bright red soda beside him, and he was now busy munching his sandwich.

'He's okay.'

'He's tied up!'

'He wanders,' she said simply. 'His mum does the best she can for him, but he's been lost before. Badly lost. Just after I came back to the island he wandered into the bush at the back of the town and we had almost every islander searching.'

'But to tie him up like that…'

'It's only ever for a few minutes,' she told him. 'And he doesn't seem to notice. Betty will have come up here for coffee with her friends. He doesn't like sitting with her inside while she chats—he gets bored and a bit…well, *grunty*… so she can't chat in peace. This is her compromise. She'd never, ever leave him for long without checking, and she always leaves him with a drink and a snack. The cord's light—if his belt's unbuckled it'll fall free so anyone can untie him, but he never tries to free himself. After being so frighteningly lost, maybe it even makes him feel safe. Most of the islanders say hi, and he seems much more content to sit and watch the world go by than he would be inside.'

She hesitated and then added, 'I know it's less than perfect, but Betty doesn't get much help. Her husband died years ago. She has a daughter, Irene, but Irene's ashamed of him.'

'We could organise more help for them.'

'We can't,' she said regretfully. 'Betty does what her daughter tells her to do, and Irene's adamant that things are okay. After he was lost I offered to organise a roster to help them. I was hoping to get Betty some time to herself, and maybe a way to give Robbie some constructive activities, but Irene got angry. "He's not worth worrying about," she told me. "He's like a dumb old dog but he's quiet. He doesn't cause trouble. Leave us be." And Betty, too... She'd been badly frightened when he was lost, but she reacted defensively. "I can look after my own son," she told me. "And if I can't then Irene will help me." I knew it was wishful thinking, but there was nothing I could realistically do.'

'Hell.'

'I know,' she said, sounding as troubled as he was. 'If there'd been medical care when he was a kid...but there wasn't. He was a teenager when I was small and I can remember him left on benches while Betty shopped even then. If he'd been treated like Noah...'

He could hear the emotion in her voice.

There must be something that could be done. He'd do it, he vowed. He glanced back at Robbie, who'd gone back to munching his sandwich—he did look content—and then the owner of the restaurant was at the door, ushering them in with huge smiles.

Angus had been treating Mario's sciatica for a month now and his pain had lessened dramatically. Freya was obviously a valued friend. The man was therefore beaming with delight, and with unabashed curiosity.

'The two of you. Together, without the little

boy. Lovely, lovely, lovely. But it's a little noisy inside here right now.' He gestured to a table of middle-aged women who looked already well into the bar menu. The group was loud and promising to get louder.

'A party,' the man said apologetically. 'Irene Veitch's birthday.' That explained the presence of Robbie outside. 'If you're happy to sit on the terrace…'

They were more than happy. Mario led them to a sheltered alcove at the side of the restaurant. The sun was hot but there was a gentle breeze, and the alcove was shaded with an overhang of gorgeous wisteria.

One lone table. A view to die for.

'Champagne?' Mario asked. 'On duty? No? I suppose one of you must be. Maybe one small champagne each to start with though, on the house, and then you can change to our home-made lemonade. A lunch without work, without the little boy… If you can't make the most of it, it won't be down to Mario Romano.'

He left them, still beaming, and Freya smiled ruefully.

'You realise this will be all over the island by nightfall. Mario sees himself as a matchmaker extraordinaire—mostly because this is the island's only decent restaurant so most couples wanting a romantic meal end up here.'

'So this is a romantic meal?'

'Cut it out. Though Mario will certainly think it is.'

Mario returned with champagne and then sidled away, subtle as a brick. Angus grinned and met Freya's eyes and found she was smiling as well. He clinked her glass with his, and then put his glass down and touched her hand. Deciding, why not be blunt?

'Freya, let's lay this on the line,' he said, gently, feeling his way. 'Your friendship is hugely important to me. We're colleagues and you're my landlady and I won't do anything that will mess with that. But the way I'm feeling now, I'd like more and if you don't… Freya, tell me to back off now.'

Her smile died. She met his gaze directly, her eyes searching. He'd known this woman for two months now and gradually, gradually the wariness had faded. The toerag who'd hurt her had done his job too well, he thought. The armour she'd built herself was fathoms deep.

But it was crumbling. Every morning, when they sat and ate toast together, every time he saw her laugh with Noah, throw Seaweed's ball, every patient they treated together and discussed together, her armour seemed to crumble even more.

She looked up at him now and he could see the almost conscious decision that the wariness had to stop. Or it had to stop if what was between them was to move any further forward.

He was holding his breath. He wasn't sure he could hold it much longer, but it seemed imperative that he try.

And then she smiled again, a different smile, wide, lovely, a smile that made him feel this was finally the real Freya. Not the Freya who'd had the stuffing kicked out of her by her rat of an ex-husband, but the lovely, laughing girl she'd once been. The Freya whose armour was disintegrating in the sunshine even while he watched. Who was placing her own champagne glass back on the table and was reaching out to touch him.

It was the most fleeting of gestures—a woman touching a man, her light fingers moulded to his face and then releasing.

'I won't tell you to back off,' she said, her voice little more than a whisper. 'Angus…maybe I don't think I can.'

The rest of the meal passed in a glorious blur. The food was magnificent, tiny platters, one after another, tasting plates exquisitely plated and presented as if each was a priceless work of art.

Which they pretty much were, Angus thought, imagining how such a restaurant would fly in Sydney. He'd never eaten such food.

Or maybe he had, it was just the day, the sun, the drooping wisteria overhead.

It was Freya.

She was laughing at something he'd said. Something silly. She was already a friend, and now there was the promise of something more. A future?

He couldn't help himself, he was envisaging barriers falling, doors between two apartments disappearing, a life together.

And the rest. Quite simply, he wanted this woman in his bed, in his life, and he wanted her now.

He'd found his woman. All the ancient primeval instincts were kicking in, the urge to pick her up and carry her back to his cave…

'Don't get ahead of yourself,' she said, and his thoughts broke off with a snap.

'What?'

But she was grinning. 'I know. If we abandoned our sweets we could possibly get home an hour before Lily brings Noah back, but Mario's chocolate soufflé has to be tasted to be believed.'

'Better than sex?'

'That,' she said serenely, 'remains to be seen. But if you don't try, you'll never find out.'

'You mean try sex?'

'Soufflé first.'

She grinned and he couldn't believe the transformation in her. Something deep within had changed.

Trust? It was there, he thought. He finally had it, this woman's trust.

Don't rush it. Don't push, he warned himself.

So with an almost superhuman effort he didn't. 'Soufflé,' he agreed gamely. 'Let's do it.'

What was she doing?

She was walking out of the restaurant and smiling like an idiot, that was what she was doing. Mario was beaming, too, and that wasn't all about the practically obscene tip Angus left. Maybe Mario's grin was because, although they weren't walking hand in hand—there was no way she was doing that in public yet—they were walking side by side, so their bodies just touched.

There was a frisson of sexual attraction she couldn't disguise from herself, and it was so strong she thought it must surely be obvious to everyone in the room. Mario certainly sensed it. His gaze was full of questions, and she knew rumours would be flying around the island already. And behind them the table of rather drunken ladies had broken off their loud partying to watch them leave.

Yep, the islanders would have her bedded and wedded by tomorrow, but did she care? Angus ushered her out into the sunshine and she felt as if she were floating in an alternate universe. A world where the impossible might just indeed be possible.

But then the door swung closed behind them—and Angus froze.

Outside was pretty much as it was when they'd entered. But the sun was stronger now, and out of the cooling of the sea breeze, the mid-afternoon heat hit them like a wave.

And with consternation, she realised Robbie was still on the bench under the tree, where they'd seen him, what, three hours ago? He was curled up as if he was resting. His empty soda bottle had fallen to the ground underneath him, where it lay beside the remains of a burst balloon. To a casual observer he was having a nap.

But while they'd been in the restaurant the sun had tracked west, and the tree's canopy was no longer shading his bench. He was still tied—and he was now in full sun.

Freya started forward in dismay, but Angus reached him before her. 'Robbie?' He put a hand on the man's head. 'Hey, Robbie?'

Robbie stirred and lifted his head to look up at them, and one look told them the worst.

His face wasn't just flushed, it was fiery red, so sunburned Freya winced in horror. He was wearing shorts, T-shirt and sandals. Every part of him that was unclothed was burned.

'Robbie…' Angus said again, and the big man's eyes tried to focus. Tears must have been tracking down his face—Freya could see their traces below his swollen eyelids.

'M-Mum…' Robbie muttered and closed his eyes.

Hell.

'Get Mario, get water, get ice,' Angus threw at her. 'And find his mum. Fast.'

He didn't have to tell her. She was already running.

She flew back into the restaurant. 'Robbie Veitch has been tied up in the sun,' she told a horrified Mario—who was still looking down in bemusement at Angus's tip. 'Since before we arrived! We need water, ice, wet cloths so we can cool him down.' She was looking wildly around the restaurant. 'Where's Betty?'

The restaurateur stared at her in horror. 'Robbie?' All the islanders knew Robbie. 'He's been out there this long?'

'Where is she?'

'Not here. It's only Irene.' He was already heading to the kitchen, shouting for wet cloths. 'They've been here for hours. If I'd known… Boys, drop everything, I want every cloth we have soaked in cold water. Tony, bring the ice bucket. Francesca, bring bottles of water. In this restaurant…in my restaurant…'

But Freya was no longer listening. She was heading towards Robbie's sister.

She'd assumed Betty was also here. She'd assumed Robbie would be cared for.

Stupid, stupid, stupid.

'Irene…' She had to yell as she reached their table. The table was littered with party detritus: opened gifts, a half-eaten birthday cake, glasses, empty and full, and champagne bottles in various stages of consumption.

Irene was seated at one end, hooting with laughter. She didn't answer as Freya reached her, and finally she had to grip her and shout in her ear.

'Irene!'

'What?' The woman was in a happy haze, and she looked around in resentment at this intrusion.

'Robbie's ill,' Freya shouted across the noise, and Irene stared in incomprehension. And then, as she recognised her, she guffawed.

'How about that?' she yelled, including the table in her discussion. 'And you a nurse. We saw you with our new doctor, and now Robbie's ill. How lucky is that? Take care of him, will you, love? See you later.'

'Irene…'

'Go away, love,' Irene said, with a drunken slur. 'If he's crook that's your job, not mine.'

Triage. Drunken relative.

She might feel sick to her stomach at Irene's response, but she had no time to waste on arguing.

Walk away.

By the time Freya got back outside the waiters had arrived with what she'd ordered. Angus had removed the cord and he and the waiters were lifting Robbie around the back of the tree and out of the sun.

'Severe heatstroke,' Angus said briefly as he saw her, and tossed her his keys. 'Grab the bag from my car.'

She felt sick.

She hadn't worried when she'd arrived and seen Robbie, apart from that constant sense of unease she always felt at Betty's form of keeping her son safe. Betty was social, often popping out for 'a cuppa with me mates', but she always kept an eye on Robbie.

Many of the islanders stopped and chatted to him when they saw him. He liked being out. Robbie seemed happy with his mum, and Betty seemed to be doing the best she could.

But Irene wasn't doing anywhere near her best. Irene never would. Rumour had it that Betty had announced she was leaving her house to Robbie when she died, and Irene was voicing disgust and anger to anyone who'd listen.

She'd thought Betty was here as part of Irene's birthday party. Why, oh, why hadn't she checked?

Because she'd been too caught up with being with Angus.

Because you lose your mind when you fall in love.

The words slammed into her head like a slap. Hadn't she already proved that was the truth?

But recriminations had to wait. She grabbed the bag from the car and returned. Robbie was lying flat on another, shaded bench. Angus was layering him with the wet cloths the staff had brought out.

He'd be like a child left in a hot car, she thought, feeling sick. The midday sun was fierce. He'd have had nowhere to escape.

And there was worse to consider. She knew his medical history.

'He has a congenital heart condition,' she told Angus and he nodded. Heart problems often went hand in hand with Down's syndrome. Robbie had had initial treatment as a child, but with the lack of medical services on the island his follow-up had been sketchy, to say the least. She handed over the stethoscope and watched Angus listen, saw his face darken.

'Can you drink, Robbie?' he asked gently. Mario handed him a water bottle. He raised Robbie's head and put the bottle to his mouth. Robbie's eyes opened but he stared upward, unseeing. Water dribbled into his mouth and then out again.

Freya grabbed ice from one of the horrified wait staff, packing it under his arms, between his legs. She told the guys to find more as she handed Angus the thermometer.

He read it and handed it to her in appalled silence, but it hadn't taken the thermometer to show just how hot Robbie was. Every inch of him that wasn't clothed was lobster red. His breathing was fast, shallow, distressing to watch.

'Get someone to lower the back seats of my car,' Angus told her. Dump Noah's car seat— we'll leave it here. Mario, can you find more towels and wet them? Anything you can. Cushions for him to lie on? We need to get him down to the clinic, get a drip in, get fluids on board. Then he'll need to be evacuated to Gannet. That heart of his…'

He didn't need to say more.

Meanwhile a small crowd was gathering. The entire wait staff had dropped everything to haul water, ice, offer any service they could. There were people watching from the doorway, patrons spilling out to get a closer look. Someone yelled back into the restaurant. 'Hey, Irene, get out here now. Robbie's real sick.'

Freya was backing Angus's SUV close to the

tree. She emerged from the car as Irene stumbled out and stopped, staring in distaste at her brother.

'What the hell do you think you're doing?' Her voice was aggressive. She was very drunk, Freya thought.

Irene was a loud and vitriolic woman at the best of times. Freya was prepared to cut her some slack—it must have been hard being brought up alongside a brother whose needs were so great—but Irene never lost an opportunity to let the world know how hard done by she'd been.

'Robbie's dangerously ill, Irene,' she said calmly now, stepping deliberately between Irene and the group—led by Angus—who'd started manoeuvring Robbie into the car. 'He was left in the sun for too long. His temperature's sky-high and he's close to collapse. We need to get him down to the clinic, get him cool, get his temperature down.'

'Let me see.'

With a doubtful look at Angus she stepped aside. Irene gazed down at her brother. 'What the hell? So he's sunburned. A bit of sun won't hurt him.'

And as if on cue, Robbie groaned and writhed. Angus signalled his carriers to put him down. They lowered him onto the grass and rolled him to his side, where he proceeded to vomit.

Except there was little to vomit. Freya glanced

back at the bench and realised this wasn't the first time he'd been sick. How dehydrated must he be?

'Just stick him back under the tree to sleep it off,' Irene told them, sounding disgusted. 'I'll take him back to Mum when he stops chucking, or ring her and tell her to get him. She might play the martyr, but I don't have to. He always does this when he wants attention.'

Freya's nails were biting into her palms. She'd been working as the island medic for over two years now and she knew Robbie had a weak stomach. His mum fed him the food she loved—cakes, sweets, and pretty much fried everything else. So, yes, there were times when Betty brought him to the clinic saying, 'He's been vomiting again.' A careful history usually elicited a story of too much fish and chips and chocolate cake, but to say this was just attention-seeking behaviour...

'Irene, this isn't just an upset tummy.' She glanced at Angus's face. His mouth was pressed into an angry line as he directed the lifters to try again. 'His temperature's sky high because of the heat, and that's causing problems with his heart. You know he has heart problems. He'll need to go to Gannet for assessment.'

'Over my dead body.'

Behind her the men had succeeded in sliding Robbie into the car. Angus was tossing the medical bag in after, then turning back to give her the keys. He'd be expecting her to drive while he stayed in the back with his patient.

'You're not taking him to Gannet,' Irene insisted. 'If his heart fails, so what? He's just a lump of lard. Mum should have got rid of him while she had the chance.'

Whoa…

'Where's your mum?' Freya was keeping a hold on her temper, but only just.

One of Irene's friends—maybe less drunk than the rest—had come up beside Irene to volunteer more information. 'Betty's home with a sore foot. Twisted her ankle or something. She pleaded with Irene to take him with us. Said he shouldn't miss out on his sister's birthday. Said he likes balloons. We even took him out one. Bloody good of Irene, if you ask me.'

'I'm always good to him,' Irene growled. 'I've been good to him my whole bloody life. Forty years… If he's got a dicky heart now, so what?'

'I'll ring Betty,' she told Angus, but the sight of his obviously controlled anger was starting to frighten her. 'I'll tell her to pack overnight gear for both of them. If her foot's not too bad she'll want to go to Gannet with him.'

'He's not going to Gannet.' Irene turned to Angus and practically shirtfronted him. 'I told you he's a wuss, and if there's something really wrong then hooray—it's about time. He shoulda been drowned at birth.'

There was a deathly silence. A silence that went on and on. Even Irene's drunken friends seemed to sense that she'd gone way too far.

Later, Freya found she'd dug her fingernails so far into her palms that they'd bled.

Anger was around them in spades. Pure unmitigated anger. She looked at Angus's face and she felt like backing away. Running.

Irene was past all control now. The horrified judgement of the onlookers seemed to be feeding her fury. Her friend was grabbing her arm, trying to drag her back, but that only seemed to infuriate her further. 'Get him out of the car and leave him.' She was spitting venom. 'Dump him, he's not worth it.'

'Get into the car, Freya,' Angus managed. 'We'll ring Betty on the way down.'

He went to climb up into the SUV beside Robbie, but Irene lurched forward again and grabbed him, hauling him around to face her. 'Didn't you hear? Leave him alone!'

From day one in their training, no matter what medical course they took, medics were taught to do everything in their power to de-escalate aggression. How to deal with drunken, drug-affected patients, their mates or their relatives. How not to rise to their bait. Please, Freya found herself pleading, though in silence in her head. Please, Angus, ignore her. Get away.

But then Irene's voice lowered to a vicious hiss. 'But hey, you've got one of these yourself, haven't you?' she spat at him. 'You probably even think his life's worth something. You're a damn fool.'

She'd been clutching his sleeve, her fingers like claws. He gripped her arms and pushed her away, and in her drunken state she stumbled and almost fell.

'You're a piece of filth,' he said, and the iciness, the loathing, the rage in his voice were a slap all by themselves. They felt like a fist in the guts, Freya thought, and as if in instant response the pain in her own gut started up again.

'You can't tell me…my own brother…' Irene was struggling to even sound coherent. 'The only good Down's is a…' And what she said then was unprintable.

Unthinkable. Unbelievable. And then she lurched forward, her fist raised. As if to hit Angus.

She didn't make it. She tripped—or maybe she simply fell—and she sprawled sideways, to lie in the grass at Angus's feet.

Angus was left staring down at her. His fists were clenched and the expression Freya saw on his face…

A memory came flooding back, uncalled for,

unwanted. She was lying on her kitchen floor. A man's livid face was looming over her, his fists clenched.

Anger, vibrating in waves, fury hitting her before he did.

A boot smashing into her. Over and over. The pain. The fear.

The loss.

It was all she could do not to vomit herself. Instead she stood perfectly still, hardly breathing, folding into herself. Trying frantically to reform the armour she'd so carefully built over the years.

Failing.

'Angus…' It was all she could do to whisper but he didn't hear. Maybe she hadn't even said it. The whole world seemed to hold its breath.

And then Angus stepped back. 'Get the car started, Freya.' His voice was loaded with flint-hard repugnance. 'Someone, look after Irene, make sure she gets home safely. Keep her away from Betty and keep her away from us. Freya, let's go.'

CHAPTER ELEVEN

MEDICAL NEED TOOK OVER. Once back at the clinic they worked together to save a life, fighting to get Robbie cool, to get his body rehydrated, to get his heart rate to settle.

Back in work mode, Freya worked on automatic pilot. She hauled out Robbie's file, flinching as she reread it.

'He was diagnosed with Tetralogy of Fallot as a baby,' she told Angus. He'd know it, the condition was high risk for kids born with Down's. 'Ventricular septal defect, narrow pulmonary valve, a big right ventricle and an enlarged aorta. Initial surgical repair went well, though.'

'Follow-ups?' Angus growled. He was focussing on adjusting oxygen.

'His mum took him back and forth to Sydney as a child, but he hasn't been since his teens. The docs from Gannet try to see him once a year—you know Marc's specialty is cardiology?—but I was here the last two times he was scheduled, and both times Irene's rung in and cancelled. She told us he hates being examined and he's fine.' She winced. 'I'm sorry, I should have followed up.'

'Don't kick yourself. I've been going through the files alphabetically and haven't reached him yet. We're both doing the best we can, and this is not our fault. But now we have every sign of heart failure. Shortness of breath, swollen legs, swollen neck veins, irregular pulse…and his colour… How much does he understand?'

'More than you'd think.' She'd talked to Robbie plenty of times over the years, and he'd seemed to understand a lot. He was barely conscious now, but Angus took his hand and gripped, leaning over so his face was in Robbie's field of vision.

'Robbie, mate, something's wrong in your middle,' he said. 'I guess it'll be hurting.' He laid his hand on Robbie's chest and left it there, a reassurance all by itself. Freya and I can't fix you here, so we're going to send you in the helicopter to the other island, to Gannet, where the special doctors are.'

Robbie's eyes widened. He looked terrified, Freya thought, and she took his other hand and nodded at Angus. Robbie knew her better than he did Angus. It might settle him to hear her speaking instead.

'Your mum's coming, and she'll be here soon,' she told him. There'd been a couple of fast phone calls when they'd first arrived. 'Right now she's packing your pyjamas, and hers, so you can be together.'

'I'll need to go, too,' Angus said softly, and she nodded.

'You and your mum and Dr Knox are going for a ride in a helicopter,' she told Robbie, and Robbie started to cry.

'Hey, it'll be fun,' she said softly. 'And your mum will be with you all the way.' And then because, dammit, she was an islander and she'd known Robbie for ever, she wiped his tears and then kept her hand on his face—she would have hugged him but there was too much medical paraphernalia in the way.

But holding him like this helped.

It helped her as well as Robbie.

Then Betty hobbled in, leaning heavily on a walking stick. She moaned with distress when she saw her son, but the moment he saw her Robbie visibly relaxed. Freya pulled over a chair, Betty took her son's head in her arms and lowered her own head, and in seconds they were cradled together.

She turned and looked at Angus and saw some of the strain clearing from his face. If ever there was proof that Robbie was loved, this was it. Freya had known it, but until this moment Angus would have had no clear idea.

Irene's vitriol had been poisonous. The hatred outside the restaurant was still making her feel ill, but this, in some measure, took away the worst of it.

But she still had work to do. With Betty here to reassure Robbie, she and Angus could move to practicalities. The chopper was about to land. 'I'll stay with him, and either take the ferry back or get the chopper to bring me,' Angus told her. 'Can you…?'

She was before him, anticipating his needs. 'Lily and I'll take care of Noah. You don't need to ask. You stay the night if you need to.'

'If there's another emergency…'

'We managed for years without you,' she said, a trifle unsteadily. 'We can manage a few more hours. Just go.'

'Freya…' He lifted a hand as if to touch her but whatever had happened over the last few hours, rational or not, she found herself backing away.

'It's okay,' she said, and she couldn't quite keep a tremor from her voice. 'Just go.'

And then they were gone. She tidied the clinic, then drove home.

Lily was on the veranda knitting, while Seaweed and Noah played in a paddling pool under a nearby tree. Noah was throwing his ball and

Seaweed was pouncing, then dropping it back into the water for a repeat.

For some reason the sight almost took Freya's breath away. Lily knitting, the little boy happy, the dog bouncing like the pup he was.

Her gut had been stabbing intermittently during the afternoon but she'd shrugged it off. She'd worry about it when she had time. Now though, as she looked at the scene before her, the pain seemed to almost double.

When she'd returned to Shearwater, this place had been her refuge. Here she could block out the pain and the helplessness of the last few years. She could rebuild and she had rebuilt. She was a strong, independent woman. Never again would she be sucked into depending, needing…loving.

Over the last few weeks her refuge had been infiltrated and her armour pierced, but this afternoon… The scene at the restaurant was like a vignette of the past, a man standing over a woman, fists clenched. The pain in her gut was like a warning.

Don't depend on anyone.

Don't lose your vulnerable heart.

'Oh, my dear.' Lily put down her knitting and came to give her a hug, maybe sensing her need, and for a moment Freya let herself be hugged. Lily was a friend. It was okay to let her barriers down here.

Or maybe it wasn't. The scene from up at the restaurant was still with her, vivid, dreadful. Irene lying in the dirt. Angus standing over her. Pure, undiluted rage.

Don't go there.

Somehow she pulled away from Lily, somehow she managed a smile. 'It's okay. We hope Robbie will be fine. He's in the best of hands.'

'I know that, dear. I've had half a dozen phone calls already telling me what happened. That Irene... I'm not sure how she'll be able to stay on the island now. Even her friends are appalled. But they tell me...you and the doctor had been drinking champagne together, they said. Oh, Freya—'

'Don't,' she said, more harshly than she meant to. 'Lily, there's nothing between us.'

'Don't talk nonsense, dear,' Lily said briskly. 'The way he's been looking at you these past weeks. He wants you, love.'

'I don't want him.'

'Really?'

'I can't. Lily, I've been married once. I can't go down that route again.'

'Why not? A ready-made family, a lovely man like Angus. Oh, my dear, it's a fairy tale.'

'Fairy tales are for books,' she managed, and the twinge in her gut suddenly jabbed again.

'Freya?' Lily's eyes creased in concern. 'What's wrong?'

'Nothing,' she denied. 'It's just…this afternoon I came close to breaking a vow, but the vow's still there. This afternoon I came very close to total stupidity.'

Lily went home. 'Call me if you need me, if you get a call-out before the doctor gets back. Or I can take Noah home with me. He likes sleeping at my place.' She gave a slightly self-conscious smile. 'You know Bernie and I had an enormous bed? Since Bernie died it's been far too big, but when Noah needs a nap at my place we nap together. Sometimes we even let Seaweed come up with us. With all of us together it feels just right.' She peeped a smile at Freya. 'Beds are so much nicer shared.'

She left and Freya put herself on automatic pilot. Her gut still hurt but she ignored it. She gave Noah dinner, popped him into bed, read him a story. She even kissed him goodnight, though that was getting close to breaking the vows that had been reforming in her head all afternoon.

She fed Seaweed and he settled down to snooze as well.

She made herself toast and tea but couldn't eat it. She sat by the fire on Angus's side of the house, needing to be there because of Noah.

She didn't want to be on Angus's side of the house.

The pain in her gut was getting stronger.

At nine at night she heard the chopper overhead. It landed on the front lawn, touching down only briefly and taking straight off again. Two minutes later Angus strode along the veranda and came in the French windows.

He saw her by the fire. 'Freya.' It was almost a caress, the way he said it, and it made her heart twist. Such a longing…

But her gut hurt, and she hurt, and she was back to operating by the set of rules she'd made herself years back.

She set down the book she'd been trying unsuccessfully to read and hauled on her professional persona.

'How did it go? How is he?'

He'd been walking across the room but now he stopped. There was something in the way she said the words…some warning. He got it, and the expression in his eyes became wary. Confused.

'He's not out of the woods yet,' he told her slowly. 'But he's in the best of hands. He's hydrated, his heart rhythm's steadied and there's every reason to be hopeful. We're lucky Marc's a top-notch cardiologist. He'll fly out with him first thing tomorrow—the evac plane's coming from Sydney. Betty's going with them. Marc thinks he'll need surgery, but the outlook's good. Now Betty's with him Robbie's completely relaxed.'

'She does love him,' she said, knowing she sounded as strained as she was feeling. 'Today... the way he was treated...it was an aberration.'

'I know that. Freya...'

'Don't.' Because he'd taken another step forward and she felt sick. The memory of that moment was all around her. She needed time, space...armour.

'What the hell?'

'It's just...' She closed her eyes. 'Sorry. It's just I seem to have an upset tummy. Too much food at lunch time—or too much excitement, I guess. I need to go to bed.'

'Love...'

'Angus, no.' She opened her eyes again and met his concern head-on. But it wasn't just concern. There was something more. Something deep, warm...wonderful?

Something that could suck her into a place she'd sworn never to visit again. Dependence. Trust.

Love?

'I can't,' she said and fought to find more and couldn't.

'You can't do what?'

Somehow she had to make him see. It was only fair. She rose and steadied, facing him front-on. 'Angus, this afternoon... The anger... You were so... I'd...forgotten...'

Somehow, he got it. His brow snapped down, confusion replaced by incredulity. 'You'd forgotten what an angry man looks like? You remembered the lowlife you married? I reminded you of him, is that what you're saying?'

'Not exactly, but—'

'Freya, do you think I could ever hit you?'

The sentence was loaded. The emotion it brought with it hung between them. There was anger behind it and she felt ill.

'I know you wouldn't.' She knew she wasn't making sense, even to herself, but there was something cold in her heart. Something dead? 'But, Angus, I need... I've learned...' She stopped, trying to regroup. Trying to sound logical. 'Angus, I need to be solitary. I know that. I can't want...'

'You can't want me?'

'No.' It was a miserable, one-syllable word and it lay between them like a block of granite.

'Because?' He sounded as if he was struggling as much as she was, only the emotions were different. Far different. 'Because I might get angry?'

'You did.'

'And you didn't?'

'Not like...you looked.'

'You're saying I looked like your ex-husband. Like the toerag who killed your baby and almost killed you. What the hell?'

'I didn't mean that!'

'Then what did you mean?'

And then another spasm hit, and she winced. It always hit when she was most stressed, and she was surely stressed right now. She gripped her middle and headed for the door. 'I need to go.'

But incredulity had given way to concern. 'Freya, you're ill.'

'I told you, funny tummy. My gut's not used to four-course lunches.' She winced. 'I'm… I'm blaming the soufflé. Sorry, Angus, I need my bathroom.'

'Let me help you.'

'No!' The word was more than a snap, it was a line he couldn't cross. 'I'll deal with this myself, thanks all the same. I don't need you, Angus.' She took a deep breath. 'I won't ever need…'

But then the pain gripped like a vice. Enough. She fled before she could finish what she wanted to say.

Except it was finished.

How could he calmly go to bed? He couldn't.

He checked on Noah, who was soundly sleeping after his busy day with Lily and Freya. Not for the first time he thanked his stars for a little boy who cheerfully accepted his circumstances. Noah loved Lily. Noah loved Seaweed.

Noah loved Freya.

Angus wasn't allowed to.

He returned to the fire and sat, staring into its depths. The events of the day were still with him, and also the anger.

Two lots of anger now. Anger with Irene for the danger she'd placed her brother in.

Anger with Freya. How could she not see that he'd never hurt her?

He understood—of course he did—but that understanding was on a logical level. A woman who'd been abused would be afraid, but to extend that fear to him…

He thought back through the events of the day, trying to put it all on a non-emotional level. Blocking out the way she'd just looked at him.

He couldn't.

She'd looked at him as if she was afraid.

He'd have to move out. He knew it, with a sickening certainty. Yes, he was attracted to Freya. He was more than attracted, he admitted to himself. She was brave, funny, caring—and sexy as hell. The way he felt about her…he wanted her, as simple as that, but he had to back off. Give her time.

How much time?

Maybe for ever…

He raked his hair and stared into the glowing embers as if he could see some solution in them. There wasn't one, at least not in the short term.

The way she'd looked at him... He wanted no woman looking like that, ever.

And right now, she was ill. Maybe her gut was coiling in a state of flight-or-fight response. If that was what he did to her...

He definitely had to give her the space she needed.

He had to get out of her home.

He headed in to check on Noah before he went to bed and found himself sitting by his son's bed, listening to his soft breathing. This place had been magical. Freya was magic.

He wouldn't leave the island, regardless of what happened. A surge of unwanted anger rose as he thought that one through. He loved it here. Noah adored Lily and vice versa. They had Seaweed. The job was great, but, feeling as he did, the situation was impossible. He needed to find another house—maybe hire someone's holiday shack until he could take up Marc's offer to find him builders.

A house somewhere near Lily? That was a no-brainer because, if he was to continue working, Noah needed Lily.

But Lily lived near Freya.

He raked his hair again and ended up with his head in his hands. What on earth could he do to persuade her he'd never hurt her?

Nothing, he thought, because the pain of what

she'd gone through was so deeply embedded that logic didn't come into it. It was bone deep and he had to respect that.

He rose and headed out to the veranda, staring out at the starlit sky. Seaweed meandered out to join him, and stared up at the sky as well. Looking for what he was looking for?

'No answers up there, mate,' he told him heavily. 'You know, in times gone by I could have got all primeval. Dragged her off to my lair, made passionate love to her, kept her under lock and key until she was damned sure I would never hurt her.'

Yeah, that made sense. Even Seaweed was looking at him as if he were a sandwich short of a picnic.

They stood there for a while, man and dog. Seaweed seemed content. Angus was just…empty.

'Cop it,' he told himself at last. A man needed to sleep—even if he knew he wouldn't. 'You have what you want,' he said out loud. 'You have the job of your dreams, a great island home, a carer for Noah who loves him to bits.'

Seaweed nuzzled his knee and Angus gave a rueful smile. 'Oh, yeah, and a dog to come home to at night. How do you feel about learning to fetch my slippers?'

Seaweed promptly plonked his butt on the

ground, looked up at him and barked. Just the once. A bark that said, 'Are you out of your mind?'

'Yeah, I can't even train you not to bite the garden hose,' he said, dredging up a smile. 'But you are what you are. Life's what it is. Chewed garden hoses and fetching my own slippers...we'll survive somehow, Seaweed. Now let's get to bed.'

He turned and went back into the house—and then stopped.

Sounds were coming from the other side of the adjoining door on Freya's side. Low moans. Pain?

The dividing door was usually locked from her side. He'd have to go around, but first he wrenched the handle.

She hadn't locked it when she'd left. The door swung inward and Freya was on the other side. She was slumped on the floor of the passage, leaning against the wall, huddled in on herself.

'Freya...'

'I'm sorry,' she whispered. 'I'm so sorry. But, Angus... My gut. I think it's adhesions. I had a ruptured bowel from...from when... Angus, I can't bear it. The pain's always been with me but now I think it's totally blocked. Angus, I'm sorry but...help me, please.'

A ruptured bowel. Adhesions. Once or twice he'd noticed Freya grimacing but she'd waved it off.

Once he'd walked into the clinic and found her holding her stomach, obviously in pain.

'Women's problems,' she'd said tersely when he'd asked, before turning instantly back into the efficient medical professional she was.

It surely was women's problems, he thought grimly, as he organised the chopper to get back here now. Or woman singular. A woman who'd been beaten so hard she'd lost her child and had her bowel ruptured. Surgical repair could often lead to adhesions, scar tissue partly blocking vital passages. It'd cause gripey pain, but surgeons would be loath to operate as more surgery could lead to more adhesions.

But she needed surgery now. Given her history, he was almost sure she was right. He didn't have the equipment to make a full diagnosis on Shearwater. She'd have to go to Gannet, and then on to Sydney. To the best damn surgeon he could find.

He gave her painkillers and organised hot packs. He made some phone calls. Then he sat in the living room with her tucked on the sofa, and he watched her do that turning into herself thing that he was starting to know so well. Starting to hate.

'I've called Lily,' he told her. 'I can go to Gannet with you.'

'I have friends on Gannet,' she whispered. 'Thanks, Angus, but they'll take care of me. Marc and Elsa on Gannet will know what to do. The only thing is…it'll leave you without a nurse.'

It'd leave him without Freya. He wanted to gather her to him, hold her. Claim her. Say to the world, this is my woman and you'll take care of her or answer to me.

He had no right. She lay huddled, dressed in the simple pyjamas he'd seen glimpses of under her kimono in the mornings in the garden.

In the morning she wouldn't be here. If they agreed on Gannet, she'd be on her way to Sydney, probably on the same evacuation flight as Robbie.

Without him. Because he had no right to go with her.

'You'll cope,' she told him, and he realised she thought he was worrying about work. He hadn't even thought about work. All his attention was on her.

Finally there was the sound of the chopper overhead. Seaweed whined and dived under the dining table.

Angus felt like whining himself. Instead he headed out to greet the medics.

Two doctors. Marc and Elsa were on board, the married couple, senior medics from Gannet. Two. It was a measure of how much this had shocked them.

It was a measure of how much Freya was valued by the islanders.

Marc went straight into handover mode but Elsa, the chief family doctor on Gannet, headed straight for Freya. And gathered her into her arms and hugged.

It was so much what Angus had wanted to do that he felt ill himself. Lost. Bereft.

She felt like his woman—and he couldn't even hold her.

Because she was afraid of him.

'You know the score,' Marc was saying. 'We'll get one of the surgeons on Gannet to look at her tonight but if what she's saying is right then it has to be Sydney.'

'Maureen Isling,' Angus growled, naming the woman with the reputation of having the best surgical fingers in Sydney. 'Only Maureen. I'll ring her tonight.'

'No, I'll ring her,' Marc said firmly. 'When we have a full clinical picture to present.'

'I know her.'

'So do I.' Then Angus found Marc's hand solidly on his shoulder and Marc was looking at him…like a friend. 'Like that, is it?'

'No. Yes. I don't know…'

'She keeps to herself, our Freya,' Marc said softly. 'You know her background?'

'Yes.'

'Then you'll have your work cut out for you, mate.' His eyes were warm with understanding.

At any other time Angus might have resented this instant jumping to conclusions but right now he was too distressed to care. 'It's not the time for that now, though,' he said sympathetically. 'We'll organise another nurse from Gannet to come over and help out. It might take a couple of days, but we'll see what we can do. You'll be all right on your own for a while?'

'Of course.'

'Great,' Marc told him, but Angus got another long, searching look before Marc turned back to the two women and started asking questions. Freya was with her friend, Elsa. She was being cared for by Marc.

There was no place for Angus at all.

CHAPTER TWELVE

WAS THERE ANYWHERE lonelier than a single room in a city hospital?

The surgery had gone 'optimistically brilliantly', Maureen had told her. The middle-aged surgeon had beamed at her as if Freya were a complex jigsaw puzzle she'd managed to complete, but now that Freya was 'solved' she hardly saw her.

The nurses were kind, caring, compassionate. She'd seen a lot of them in the twenty-four hours post op but two days later they were busy with other cases, and apart from routine obs she was left alone. She was due to head to a rehab ward tomorrow for a few more days before she was permitted to return to the island.

'Not that I don't think you'll be fine,' Maureen had told her when she'd objected. She'd wanted to go straight home. 'I defy any bug to mess with my work, but it's best to be safe. The Birding Isles are too damned far. If there's to be any complication, I want you under my watch.'

So she was stuck here, and after tomorrow she'd be stuck in a rehab ward. She shifted in her bed and winced—the stitches still pulled. It was mid-afternoon. She could hear laughter, voices, kids in the corridor—the sound of visitors on a Saturday afternoon in a big hospital.

Once upon a time she'd had lots of friends in Sydney. She'd done her training here, she'd even had fun. For a while. But a manipulative, controlling husband had quietly set about isolating her, and she'd been too naive to fight. Until it had been far, far too late.

And right now it was hard not to feel sorry for herself. Maureen had done her repair work. 'There may well be more adhesions down the track. I'm not a miracle worker,' she'd admitted. 'But we'll get onto them early. Don't you dare leave them again until you get yourself in this state.' Maureen was setting up an annual check, 'just to make sure'. So her pain was over. Her loneliness had an end point. In a few days she could head back to her island, head back to her life.

Without Angus. Which meant a whole new level of loneliness.

He was still her colleague, she reminded herself, but he couldn't be her tenant. Not now. She'd have to tell him. The way she felt—no, the way *he* felt, she reminded herself—it'd be playing with fire to have him living so close to her.

If she could just be brave enough...

But she was here because once upon a time she had been brave, falling in love with romance, with a guy who'd charmed her socks off.

'And I'm no longer so completely stupid,' she said out loud to the empty room. 'To depend on someone...to let someone control my life like that...'

'He wouldn't,' she contradicted herself.

'That's what you thought about Craig.' She lay back on the pillows and deliberately forced her mind back to the heady days when she'd first met the man who'd become her husband. The instant sexual attraction—he was ten years older than her, knowledgeable, decisive, sure. The way he'd smiled at her, edging her away from a group of fellow trainee nurses so he could get to know her better. The feeling of being cherished, cared for, desired...

The slow realisation of control. The dawning recognition of her mistakes.

She stared out of the window at the rectangle of sky she could see from her tenth-floor window and swiped away a trickle of a stupid tear.

'Stupid, stupid, stupid,' she muttered, and of course—because when could you ever get away with stupidity without consequences?—there was a knock on the door.

It would be a nurse for obs, she thought—or, given her luck, a pastoral care worker. Someone who'd see the trace of tears and pounce. Empathy-plus. She didn't need it.

She swiped her face again and called, 'Come in,' with a whole lot more aggression than was even remotely called for—and the door opened and it was Angus. And Noah.

Her two favourite people in the whole world.

Noah was clutching the most enormous bunch of flowers she'd ever seen. It was a rainbow of fragrant colour, a massive assortment of flowers which looked as if they'd been plucked from a cottage garden ten minutes ago. The bunch practically enveloped Noah's small body as he stomped into the room—a man on a mission—and thrust the flowers onto her bed.

'Faya,' he said, in a tone that said this had been rehearsed. 'Get better.'

She gazed down at his earnest little face and it might sound corny—it was a phrase she would have scorned until now—but her heart melted, right there and then. And then she looked up at the man who'd followed him in, and the corny phrase faded into insignificance. It wasn't vast enough.

No phrase could be vast enough.

'Hey,' he said and smiled at her, and if that wasn't enough to set her off…

She wouldn't cry. *She would not cry.*

'Hey, yourself,' she managed, and it was a wonder she could get the words out at all. 'I… What… How…?'

But he at least was under control, still smiling but ready to explain. He lifted the flowers from where they lay on top of her breast—as if she were a corpse?—and laid them on her tray. And then he touched her cheek. A brush of fingers on skin. A feathertouch.

'We had to come.'

Her heart was hammering so hard it was a wonder it wasn't visible from the outside. 'But the island… Our patients…'

He was smiling right at her, a caress all by itself. Oh, that smile…

'When I started working on Shearwater it was on the condition that I'd need breaks,' he told her. 'I was thinking it'd be because Noah might well need treatment on the mainland, or his mother might eventually want access. I didn't think it'd be because I needed to be with someone I've learned to care about so much I couldn't stay away from her.'

There was enough in that to take her breath away.

She couldn't let it. Focus on practicalities, she

told herself desperately. Focus on something other than that smile!

'You shouldn't have,' she managed. 'To leave Shearwater without either of us…'

'Irresponsible, isn't it?' he told her, and his smile deepened. 'But it seems almost the entire population of Shearwater—no, make that the entire population of the Birding Isles—care about you. Deeply. Someone had to come and check on you, and Noah and I were elected.'

'But if something happens there…'

'Then Marc and Elsa will take care of things,' he told her. 'They've come over from Gannet and are staying in your house. I hope that's okay, by the way. They'll stay for a week, and if you need me here for longer then they'll organise that, too. Medically, the islanders are safe.'

'But you don't need to stay for a week!' It was all she could think of, but even as she said it she thought: who knew why he was here anyway? He could be here for Noah's needs, or for something else entirely.

But then, what had he said? *If you need me here for longer…*

'I figured you'd be alone,' he said simply. 'And I couldn't bear it. Neither could Noah when I explained. I told him you were sick and you needed a friend. We packed together.'

'Seaweed?' How dumb was she sounding? She

was clutching at straws, swerving from anything personal.

'Lily has Seaweed in hand. Last time we saw her she was leading him happily to her place, planning out loud how many dog biscuits he'd need for a week's stay.'

'Angus...'

'Freya, I couldn't stay away,' he said simply, and then, having had enough of words, he lifted Noah to the side, bent over and kissed her.

It wasn't a kiss of passion. It was a kiss of... she didn't know what. Tenderness? Friendship? An invitation to step into a space that still had her terrified?

But for a moment she allowed herself to stay in that space, to feel the brush of his lips on hers, to savour the strength of his hands cupping her face. She felt herself melting into his smile as he pulled back—still cupping her face—as he searched her eyes.

'How goes it, my Freya?'

My Freya. It was a reminder, a stab to the gut and he saw it.

'No,' he said, too quickly, fast enough for her to realise he'd seen the panic. 'That was daft. You're not my Freya. I hope, though, that you're still my friend.' He searched her face, and he must have seen the track of that lone tear because his finger traced it. 'Are you in pain?'

'N…no pain. Maureen's been amazing.' She fought to sound impersonal. Medical. 'Everything's in working order again. She can't guarantee no more adhesions, but she'll be on top of them before they become a problem. She makes it clear she'll regard any such problems as a personal affront.'

'She's great,' Angus said warmly, and tugged up a chair and hitched Noah onto his knee. 'Can I tell you our plan?'

'Your plan.' She was at sea here, feeling dazed.

'Maureen and Noah and me,' he said, a trifle smugly. 'We make a great team.'

'You've been talking to Maureen about me?'

'Maureen was a consultant here when I was an intern,' he told her. 'That was how I knew how good she was. She felt free to yell at me when I did something silly as a student. Now, as your referring doctor, I had the temerity to ring and ask how you were going, and she yelled at me all over again.'

This conversation was getting away from her. She was feeling winded. Spinning a little.

It's the painkillers, she told herself, but she knew it wasn't the drugs.

'So why would she yell at you?' It was all she could do to get the words out, but she felt inordinately pleased that she managed it.

'She told me she'd booked you into rehab because there's nowhere else for you to go. So if I cared about you…'

'You can't care.' She was fighting to find a boundary, but it wasn't working.

'Friends do care,' Angus said gently, and once again his hand came out and his fingers traced that damned tear track. 'Freya, we've agreed I'll back right off. I will not pressure you, not now, not ever. But neither will I sit back and let you be alone. Just before my father died he bought a house, small but beautiful, overlooking the harbour. He had it fitted for disability in case he needed it as he got older. As it happens, he dropped dead in the midst of a rambunctious night out with his mates, and he left it to me. Noah and I used it…after we left Deb. We should have put it up for sale, but we were waiting to see how Shearwater worked out first. So here's our proposition. Instead of rehab you use our house and Noah and I will stay on for a few days as your carers. And,' he added gently, 'I hope, as your friends.'

'I don't…' She was practically stuttering. 'I don't need carers.'

'Maureen says you do, and we're up for the job. We're good at cooking for ourselves, aren't we, Noah? And we can easily extend that cooking to three. But if you don't like our cooking, you have no idea of the take-out options in Sydney. Compared to Shearwater, they'll blow your mind.'

'But I can't.' The panicked response was out before she could stop it, and Angus's smile died.

'Are Noah and I so scary?'

'No. Yes! Sorry. Angus, it's just the way I feel.'

'Like you don't trust my cooking?'

'You know I do, but…'

'I know,' he said gently. 'It takes courage to trust, but, for now, Noah and I are asking you to find that courage. For friendship, nothing more. Freya, I promise there will be no pressure. Noah and I have people we need to catch up with in Sydney. Noah would like to see his mum, and there are people I'd like to get together with, too. There are lots of things that'll keep us out of your hair. But the house is superb. We have a sun-drenched balcony overlooking the harbour. We have a swimming pool—I've paid to keep it maintained. There's a library full of books and a sound system to die for. All you need to do is lie in the sun and get better.'

'And trust.' She said it before she could stop herself.

'And trust,' he said evenly, and stood, lifting Noah with him. 'But that's up to you, and we'll leave you to decide. Noah and I just got off the plane. We came straight to you, but our plan is to head to the harbour now and find mango ice cream. The things you miss living on Shear-water… I'll come in later tonight and hear your decision.'

'Angus, you shouldn't… I can't.'

'I think you can,' he said gently. 'I know you value isolation above all else, but right now you need help. Noah and I think you need us. Freya, your courage to trust is in there somewhere. I know it's been bashed to a pulp but it's still there. All you need to do is find it. Noah, would you like to kiss Freya on the nose and say goodbye?'

'Yes,' Noah said, and Angus lowered his son, who dutifully kissed Freya on the nose.

'Bye-bye, Faya,' he said, and they were gone.

Then Maureen arrived.

So much for a quiet Saturday afternoon. An hour ago she'd been desperately lonely, and now she was desperately…discombobulated.

Usually when she saw Maureen, the consultant was trailed by an attendant nurse or a following of students. Now she was alone. She was dressed in a scarlet jogging suit and a crimson bandana, looking as if she'd just completed a run. She was pretty much the opposite of the brisk professional Freya had been seeing over the last couple of days.

She knocked and came in without permission—since when did consultants ever ask permission? But consultants usually checked charts and moved straight to either examination or medical interrogation. Maureen did neither.

She sat and searched Freya's face and then gave a decisive nod. 'So he's been?'

'Angus?'

'Who did you think I meant?' Maureen was a woman of few words, brisk, efficient, smart.

'You knew he was coming?'

'Of course I knew. And I've figured out why, and so I've decided you should know,' she said. Decisively. Clearly a woman on a mission.

'Freya, I've known Angus since he was eight years old,' she continued, before Freya had a chance to stop her. 'Back then I was an intern in the paediatric ward, and he was admitted with sarcoma. Lower leg. Caught early, thanks be, but I remember him as the bravest kid. Mostly because he was in for a while and his parents hardly came near him. His nanny had found the lump on his leg—his parents were on a safari in Africa and they didn't get home until a week after diagnosis. Poor little soul. So...

'So I was at the end of my rotation and I ended up spending a bit of time with him. He was smart, interested, asking every question under the sun. I enjoyed him, the feeling seemed to be mutual, and when his treatment stopped he used to write to me. Mostly it was medical questions—his illness was probably the start of his journey to his career—but I enjoyed those letters. When he started med training I saw a bit more of him. Maybe he sees me now as a kind of meddling aunt, and I probably am. When he married… Well, I knew Deborah and her family, and I told him what I thought. Things cooled between us for a while after that. Call that meddling? I couldn't help myself, but does anyone ever listen to their elders' advice? I don't think so.'

Freya was bemused. But also stunned. One word stood out.

Sarcoma.

Bone and soft tissue tumour.

Angus at eight years old, with a life-threatening disease.

She was suddenly thinking back to being in the surf with him, with that scar running down the side of his leg. She'd seen him with a surfboard, she'd spotted the scar and she'd made an assumption. She'd been so wrong.

Sarcoma was a malignant cancer. He'd been lucky not to have lost his leg. And his life.

'He got the best treatment,' Maureen told her, obviously following her line of thought. 'His parents were good at throwing money at problems, but as for hands-on caring… Anyway, that's past now, and so's his marriage. I was pleased as punch when he told me he was going to Shear-water.'

'Should you be telling me this?' Freya asked.

'Yes, I should,' she insisted firmly. 'Because I'm sure as eggs that he won't tell you, and the way he feels about you…'

'How do you know…?' She broke off but she didn't have to continue.

'Because he told me. Oh, not in so many words. I've been ringing him periodically—did you know Noah's my godson? It was therefore my duty to check, and even Noah's managed to get the gist across to me—how much the pair of them have been falling in love with Noah's *Faya*.'

'In love,' she repeated faintly.

'I'm not dumb. He's nutty about you. The night you collapsed he rang and practically ordered me to meet the plane. It was killing him that he couldn't come with you, that he had to wait until someone else arrived to take over the medical needs of Shearwater. And of course he's been on the phone ever since, demanding I do every-thing in my power to take care of you. But he's said enough for me to figure there was a prob-lem between the two of you, and as your treat-ing doctor I now know your history. I've seen the mess that toerag made of your body.' Her bossy tone softened and she met Freya's gaze front-on.

'Freya, I've treated abused women before, and I know how hard it must be to trust again.'

'Maureen—'

'No, I just want you to listen,' Maureen told her. 'In a way this is none of my business except I would love a happy ever after for my godson— but I do want to tell you what Angus will never tell you himself.'

'I shouldn't—'

'And neither should I,' Maureen interrupted. 'But I've just had my Saturday run and I ran my legs off and in the end there was this beat running with me. Tell her, tell her, tell her. So here goes. You have an issue with trust? Of course you do. Freya, I'm your surgeon and I've seen for myself what's been done to you in the past. But I'm here to tell you that Angus could no sooner hurt you—or hurt anyone—in any way possible, than he could fly.'

'I know that.'

'In your head you might,' Maureen told her. 'But in your heart? Or in your gut, which that bastard's so damaged?' She leaned over and gripped Freya's hand. 'Listen.'

'I'm listening.' She was feeling numb. She wanted Maureen to stop—there was no way this could help—but Maureen seemed unstoppable.

'The day Angus decided his marriage was

over… I've never seen anyone more consumed with anger in my life.'

This was none of her business. She should say it—but the image came again of Angus, standing over Irene. His fists clenched. His face tight with rage. 'I can imagine.'

'No, you can't,' Maureen said bluntly. 'You weren't there, but I was. Freya, there was a huge charity event, a hospital fundraiser, held in a massive marquee on the harbour front. Anyone who was anyone was there. Tickets were like gold. And of course Deborah—Angus's wife—was one of the society ladies who'd helped organise it. I was there because they needed a smattering of senior staff to schmooze the big givers. Angus was there because he had to be, as Deborah's husband. It was a Sunday lunch, seven courses, international guest speakers, lavish decorations. A vast success. And towards the end, in comes Noah's au pair, carrying Noah.'

'Uh oh,' Freya said, because that was all she could think of. 'I mean… I guess…'

'Don't guess,' Maureen snapped. 'I'll tell you. It seemed Deborah had decreed nothing was to interfere with her event—she was pretty much owning it. And so she'd not only turned her own phone off, she'd managed to switch Angus's phone to silent as well. Without telling him. It seems Noah had had a febrile convulsion and had been vomiting for hours. I learned later the au pair was new—Deborah had sacked the last one. She was also not too bright. Instead of taking him to the hospital, she'd caught a taxi to where she knew his parents were.

'So in she comes, and she sees Deborah first, blindingly obvious on the head table. I'm not sure if I can paint a word picture here but imagine. Deborah's dress was pure white, with tiny embroidered diamantés making her shimmer when she moved. Her hair was piled in the most elaborate chignon. *She* looked stunning, but even from where I sat I could tell she was more than a little tipsy. And then up marches the au pair and presents her with her child. A little boy, three years old, wan, ill, smelling of vomit. Worse, a little boy with Down's syndrome, a fact Deborah had tried to keep secret from society, a little boy who'd caused her nothing but shame. And the au pair, who by this time had had enough, thrust Noah straight at her. She said: "This is the last time you tell me I can phone if something's wrong and you don't answer." And she leaves.'

'Oh, no!'

'I was on one of the front tables,' Maureen told her. 'As a senior hospital representative. But Angus, as a mere husband, was seated up the back. He'd seen them arrive, but it took time for him to thread through the tables to reach them.

So she was left holding him, her face rigid with mortification. That look…you can't imagine. If the photographers from the society tabloids had seen they would have had a field day.

'I guess my first reaction was to protect them, well, to protect Noah. So I reached them before the cameras did, and managed to steer them behind one of the screens beside the stage. Then, just as Angus reached us, Noah retched again. He didn't even vomit, poor little chap—he was past having anything in his tummy. Just a tiny bit of bile. But Deborah practically threw him at me with disgust. Then Angus reached them, and she screeched. I can still hear her. She was over the top with fury, drunk and mortified.

'"Get it out of here," she commanded as he got within earshot. "I won't let you and your imbecile son ruin my day." Then she looked down at her dress and saw the stain, and as Angus reached her—she hit him.'

'Oh, God…'

'Indeed, my dear,' Maureen said. 'And Angus's face… I've never seen him look like that, and I hope never to see it again. *Get it out of here.* The words seemed to be echoing round and round the marquee, so loudly I was sure others must have heard. It never reached the tabloids but I don't know how. I was holding Noah, watching Angus's anger, his shock, waiting for… I don't know what. But Angus simply reached out and lifted Noah to him, hugged him close, murmured something for his ears only and then turned back to Deb.

"'I'm sorry we've messed with your day," he said, almost gently. "Maureen, could you ask a waiter to find a cloth to wipe my wife's dress? Noah, we're going home. Excuse us, please."

'And then he walked out without a backward glance, and Deb went to the bathroom and wiped off her dress and came back and drank more champagne and pretended nothing had happened. I gather Angus moved himself and Noah into his father's house that night and that was the end of their marriage. She's been bad-mouthing him ever since but he's stayed silent. He's even tried to encourage Deb to still see Noah.

'So there you are. It's a horrid story and it's probably best forgotten, except I'm telling you, Freya, that if trust is your issue then forget it. Angus stood in that marquee, his face red from the vicious slap Deb gave him, and all he cared about was getting his little son out of there. He even found it within him to be gentle with a wife he must once have loved, and he carried Noah out, cradling him like he was the most precious thing in the world.'

At that Maureen paused. She sniffed, and the

curt professional suddenly had tears glistening behind her eyes.

'I've been lucky in my marriage, my dear,' she said, softly now, and she reached out and covered Freya's hand with hers. 'And I know what a gift it is to be loved by such a man. Freya, I know you're scared, and I of all people should know why. But the first time he saw you, Angus told me you'd saved a dog. He said you were courage personified. So, Freya dear, if you can find courage to save a drowning dog, please think about finding the courage to save Angus.'

'He doesn't need saving.'

'No? Because he's a male, because he's wealthy, strong, sure? Because he stands up for his son? Because you think he doesn't need you? I saw him when he was eight, alone in his hospital bed, listening in on the scary things the doctors were saying. Freya, that scared kid is still in there. I'm not saying you should love him for that. I'm just saying, there's more than one person in this equation who needs to find the courage to trust. So,' she said gently. 'That's all I wanted to say. Think about it, my dear. I'll leave you now to do just that.'

He came late, just as visiting hours were about to end. He was as she'd first seen him, dressed in casual chinos and a short-sleeved open-neck shirt. His hair was ruffled. He didn't have Noah with him.

He looked…like Angus. Like the man who made her heart turn over.

But he also looked different. Was she seeing inside him, to the child Maureen had told her about? To a man she'd judged against a violent norm that had nothing to do with him?

'Hey,' he told her, and he crossed straight to the bed and kissed her. Lightly, on the hair. It was a kiss of greeting, nothing more. 'I'm sorry I'm late. Maureen and her husband are babysitting, and Noah took a while to settle. Maureen's husband's an academic, a lovely man but not exactly intuitive. He dropped the news that I was coming back to see you, so it took three full readings of Noah's favourite story book to make him so sleepy he forgot to insist on coming too.'

'That'd be *Where Did the Wombat Lose His Tail?*,' she said, remembering Noah clutching his best book, and she smiled, and he smiled back, and suddenly they were grinning at each other like idiots.

Like a man and a woman who'd known each other for ever.

Like a family?

'Maureen came to see me,' she managed.

'She told me.'

She searched his face. His expression was non-committal. Waiting.

'She told me about your marriage,' she ventured, because it had to be said. 'And about your leg. I'm… It made me ashamed.'

She saw his face close a little. 'She had no right.'

'Don't you dare yell at her. She's great.'

'She is but she's—'

'A meddling aunt. She told me.'

He smiled again at that, a trifle ruefully. 'She is that. But don't believe any hard luck tale she tells you. I've been lucky.'

'Really?'

'Yes,' he said, forcefully now. 'I have. But that's nothing to do with here and now. Freya, will you come to my father's house for your convalescence?'

'Yes, please,' she said because there was nothing else to say.

He didn't move. He stood, looking down at her, his expression inscrutable.

'So… What Maureen said… You're not agreeing to come because you feel sorry for me?'

It was so much the opposite of what she'd been thinking that she almost gasped. 'No! How can I feel sorry for you?'

'The same as I can't feel sorry for you, I guess.

Moving forward... You'll come as my guest? No pressure?'

'No pressure,' she said, and she wanted to reach up and take his face in her hands and draw him down and kiss him.

She couldn't.

No pressure.

She was suddenly unsure. In uncharted territory.

'You know this is friends only,' Angus said, almost sternly, and as he stepped back she wondered if it was entirely accidental that he'd come at the end of visiting hours, when there was no time for further discussion between them. 'I will not push you past the boundaries you need to have in place. I've accepted that and I've planned accordingly.'

'Planned...'

'Because pressure is the last thing either of us wants,' he told her. 'Freya, I have a great life. I have a job I love, in a place I love. I have my son and I have a dog, and I'm not about to let what seems...what *seemed* to be happening between us mess with that. In the couple of days before I came here I made enquiries and there's a house for rent right near the clinic. I've organised to take it until my own house is built on the island. We have this week together, with Noah and I doing the caring, but we're assuming nothing going forward. No matter what Maureen said, I need no sympathy, and, I suspect, neither do you. So… friends?'

'F…friends,' she whispered, a trifle unsteadily, and he smiled. He bent and kissed her again, but once again it was the kiss of a friend.

'Right,' he told her briskly, moving on. 'Discharge is at ten tomorrow. Noah and I will be here to collect you. Sleep well, Freya, and we'll see you in the morning.'

She nodded, mutely—and then he was gone.

He walked back through the corridors, then into the elevator with a group of departing visitors. There was a particular kind of silence among them. They were all leaving, with friends or loved ones staying behind.

How many times had he seen this, visitors arriving and leaving? He stood now within the group of seven or eight silent people, and he wondered if they were feeling as he was.

As if he'd left part of himself behind.

Freya.

How had he fallen for her so hard?

But he understood her fears. Maureen had spelled out the damage that had been done to her. That was probably unethical, but he was her referring doctor. Almost. He should back away from that, he thought. Doctors shouldn't treat family.

Was she family, though?

No. She was simply the woman he'd fallen in love with. When? How? Was it when she'd dived overboard to save Seaweed? Or the moment he'd helped drag her aboard? Was it when he'd first seen her laugh with Noah—or the time she'd motioned to where the ashes of her tiny daughter lay buried in her beautiful garden?

Who could say when love happened? He only knew that he had, and if it took years to gain her trust…

He smiled at that, ruefully, imagining himself growing old with Noah and Seaweed, while Freya got on with her life with…

'Nobody.' He said it out loud and the people in the elevator looked at him curiously and then they reached the ground floor and they edged out around him.

'The psych department's in a separate building,' he wanted to assure them, but he didn't.

What he did say to himself as he walked out into the night was more to the point.

'I have to give her time,' he said. 'No pressure, Angus Knox. You need to back off, for however long it takes.

CHAPTER THIRTEEN

THERE COULDN'T BE a more perfect place to recuperate in the known world.

She still ached. Her body was taking its own sweet time, but there was nothing for her to do here but get better. She lay on the sun lounger beside the pool at Angus's father's house and looked out over Sydney harbour and thought that this was the stuff of dreams.

What was even more wonderful was that she was pretty much waited on hand and foot by Angus. And Noah.

But they didn't invade her personal space. The pair were around at meal times, and at Noah's nap time, but during Noah's naps Angus shut himself into his father's office and worked. The rest of the time they seemed to be busy.

'Effenants,' Noah said triumphantly to her after she'd been there for five nights.

She'd been feeling so good she'd offered to cook, but she'd been howled down.

'Noah and I have planned spaghetti,' Angus

had told her, so she'd sat at the kitchen table and watched father and son make dinner.

Then Noah looked up from the plate of 'worms' he'd been inspecting and beamed. 'Effenants,' he repeated, forcefully. 'Tigells.'

'You've been to the zoo?' she ventured.

'Mombats,' Noah added as a clincher, and went back to devouring his spaghetti.

'Fun?' she asked, and Angus grinned.

'Really fun. We're going to the museum tomorrow, but I doubt dinosaur bones will match it.'

She shouldn't ask but she couldn't help herself. 'Have you seen Noah's...?' She glanced at Noah and rephrased. 'Have you seen Deb yet?'

His face closed. 'Deb's packing to head overseas with her new partner.'

'She's too busy to see you?'

Noah was holding up a strand of spaghetti and lowering it inch by inch into his mouth. Totally absorbed. Not interested in the grown-up talk.

'Of course she's too busy,' Angus said shortly. 'I should have expected it. As far as she's concerned the pregnancy was a mistake, to be put behind her as fast as possible.'

'Oh, Angus.'

'I'll make it up to him. Somehow.' He added a handful of chopped olives, basil and roasted pine nuts to the basic sauce he'd given Noah. 'There you are, my lady. The chefs of this world can eat their hearts out.'

She chuckled and turned her attention to her meal.

'I'm thinking if you feel well enough to stay here by yourself, then Noah and I will go home on Saturday,' he said, and suddenly her pasta didn't taste so good.

'Of course,' she told him brightly. 'I'm getting better and better. I can go back to work next week.'

'Not so soon. Take another week here, then a couple of weeks sleeping in your garden.'

Two weeks in her garden. Before Angus had come she would have killed for such an opportunity. As Shearwater's only medic she'd been pushed to the limit. Now, though, she thought, the garden will be empty. She might eventually go back to having the occasional paying guest, but the rest of the time the garden would be hers, to enjoy in solitude.

Without Noah and Seaweed.

Without Angus.

'You don't have to move out.' She said it quickly and then flushed. 'I mean…'

'I think we do.'

'Angus…'

'Freya, I can't be near you and not want you.'

Oh.

Oh, oh, oh.

The silence between them then was almost deafening. Say it, her heart was screaming. Say that you want him, too. More, say that you need him. Say how desolate life will be once he leaves.

But...

There was always a but. The *but* had been in-stilled into her, kicked into her, grieved into her.

How many years had she spent telling herself that she needed no one? Shut up, she told herself sharply, and it felt like stabbing herself.

'I'll make dinner tomorrow night,' she said, standing abruptly and taking her bowl to the sink.

'You haven't eaten.'

'I'm not hungry.'

'Because of what I just said.'

'No.' She hesitated. 'Yes.'

He nodded, serious, thoughtful. Figuring what she needed? Then he rose and took her pasta bowl from by the sink, carrying it out to the balcony. Then he came back, picked up her glass of wine and carried it out as well. And did the same with her cutlery and napkin. He set it all down on the outdoor setting-dinner for one.

'There's your dinner,' he told her. 'The night's warm, the balcony's lovely and if you eat by your-self your stomach won't clench.'

'How do you know it was?'

'I can guess. Freya, we all do what we need to do. You need to survive, and if it takes solitude for that to happen then that's what has to be. So you head outside and eat in peace. Noah and I will finish our pasta in here. Then I'll read Noah a bedtime story and go to the study to do some work. So we'll say goodnight now.'

And then he took her shoulders and gently propelled her out to the balcony.

'Say goodnight to Freya,' he told Noah, and Noah lifted his spaghetti-laden fork and waved.

'Bye-bye, Faya,' he said as Angus pulled the big glass doors closed behind her.

Freya did what she was told. She ate in isolation. She drank her wine and then she moved across to her sun lounger. Inside, the living room lights were switched off. Angus and Noah had disappeared.

The night was still and warm. When she'd first arrived Angus had loaded the sun lounger with pillows and rugs. She hardly needed them during the day, but now she snuggled underneath and tried to stop shivering.

She was shivering because…

Because my body's recovering from surgery, she told herself, but she knew it was no such thing. Nor was she shivering because she was cold.

She felt like a coward.

Somewhere inside Angus would be reading

his umpteenth rendition of *Where Did the Wombat Lose His Tail?*

He was a nice man.

No. She closed her eyes and let herself see Angus as she'd seen him over the past two months. Angus, helping her save the dog, taking Seaweed into his home, into his life.

Angus performing a tracheotomy, reassuring, skilful, sure.

Angus freeing a toe from a tap. Trying not to laugh.

Angus in the surf, holding his little son on his surfboard. Angus with a scar she'd thought had been caused by misadventure but, instead, was caused by trauma. Childhood fear and loneliness.

He wasn't a 'nice' man. He was so much more.

'He deserves someone better than me,' she whispered.

'But he wants me.'

'And I want him!'

'So what's stopping you?'

She lay and watched the reflected lights of the famous bridge mingle with the moonlight over Sydney harbour. Far out past the harbour entrance lay Shearwater, her home, her sanctuary, the place she'd run to.

As Angus had run?

'No. He belongs on Shearwater. It's his home as well as mine.'

She said the words out loud, trying to settle the crazy fluttering in her chest. It almost felt like a panic attack, she thought. Why couldn't she settle?

'Because he's going home without me. Because by the time I get home he'll already have another home.'

'It'll only be down the road.'

'But still…'

The night drifted on, warm, peaceful. A late ferry was chugging across the harbour, leaving glittering phosphorescence in its wake.

Then another image superimposed itself. Angus, the day at the restaurant. Irene's vitriol. Her vicious slap and then her fall. Angus looking down at her, his fists clenched, his face white with anger.

And Angus turning away to deal with the things that mattered. To a man who'd been hurt. To medical need, but, more, to emotional need.

He was a man who'd turned away from venting his anger to do what he had to do.

She stood up and walked to the balcony rail and thought, What can I possibly be afraid of?

She considered Angus and what he'd gone through in the past, and she thought, He has so much more reason to distrust me. And yet…

'Freya, I can't be near you and not want you.'

His words echoed around and around in the

still night air. What a statement of trust. What a leap of faith.

Angus.

Angus and Noah and Seaweed. A package deal.

Suddenly there came hope, like a lightning bolt that split her carefully built armour, and it hit so hard, so fast that she almost staggered. In that one blinding flash she thought: who needed courage when a man like Angus said, *'I can't be near you and not want you.'*? She stayed quite still, expecting it to go, but instead it steadied. Settled.

It was no longer a lightning bolt. It was coalescing into warmth, gratitude, certainty.

Love?

Yes, she thought. Yes!

So what next? Go inside now and tell him she'd been blind?

No. It needed to be a statement. A big statement.

Once, a long time ago when she was a student in Sydney, she'd been lying on the famous Bondi Beach when a small plane had flown low, the length of the beach. Behind it had fluttered an enormous banner, words red against white, hearts surrounding vivid lettering.

'Jessie, Will You Marry Me?'

She remembered looking around at the crowded

beach, as everyone was, to see if they could spot 'Jessie', but she'd wondered at the same time how many Jessies were on the beach; how many guys beside their Jessies were stuttering, 'Not me, not me.'

So not a plane, she thought. But what?

She turned away from the view and her stitches pulled, the twinge reminding her that she was still convalescing. So there went her second idea— which actually had been pretty much her first— heading inside right now and jumping his body. It was a pretty enticing prospect—no, make that very enticing. But, dammit, she wouldn't do it if the first touch made her yelp.

He'd understand.

Yeah, but I don't want understanding, she thought. I just want him.

She looked down at her empty pasta dish and her wine glass, and something Angus had once said slipped back into her head. *You have no idea of the take-out options in Sydney. Compared to Shearwater, they'll blow your mind.* She looked again out at the harbour, then at the gorgeous outdoor setting, the balcony in the moonlight. Okay, no jumping, but as far as moving forward…as far as matching his courage with a bit of her own…

Who needed aeroplanes and banners? She had everything she needed right here.

* * *

At the entrance to the museum there was a display of 'evolution'. For some reason it included slater beetles—tiny grey creatures busily working their way through a tank of gravel and dirt. Angus would have walked straight past, but Noah was hooked.

He followed his dad, though. He politely looked at the enormous dinosaur skeleton towering over their heads, at the rest of the major exhibits Angus thought would have appealed, and then he tugged him back to the beetles.

The tank was almost at floor level. Noah proceeded to lie on his stomach and watch. He was entranced.

He continued to be entranced for a very long time.

Which gave Angus time to think. Things he found hard to think about. Like going back to the island and moving out of Freya's house. Like not seeing Freya every morning in her garden. Like her being alone with her demons.

But there was nothing he could do. If he could single-handedly wrestle her demons then he would, but he'd offered as much as he could. The rest was up to her.

Maybe there never would be a way. He sat on as Noah gazed at the bugs and he thought, Maybe she's right to hold back. He was a package deal, linked for ever to his little boy with special needs plus, it seemed, one dopey dog with an unfortunate urge to dig up seedlings.

She'd probably be better off without him.

She wouldn't. He knew she definitely wouldn't, but there was nothing he could do about it. Even staying here longer…she was starting to feel the strain of them being so close and so was he. He should never have told her what he felt.

He glanced at his watch. Three o'clock. Too early to go home yet. He needed to give her space.

'Let's go catch a ferry,' he told Noah. They could catch one of the longer ferry rides. He could gaze at the scenery while Noah napped.

Yeah, as he was gazing at the scenery right now. He'd still think about Freya.

This was his last day, he told himself. Tomorrow he'd head back to Shearwater and get his life in order. Without Freya.

'Come on, Noah,' he told him. 'Enough bugs. Let's go.'

'Home,' Noah said, struggling to his feet. 'Faya.'

'Not yet,' Angus told him and then thought with a wince, maybe not ever.

They arrived just before six, and she'd finished. She was fighting nerves, but she'd done all she could. She stood on the balcony and surveyed her handiwork with satisfaction.

It was stunning what could be achieved at the

end of a phone. An hour of calls and repeating over and over the details of her credit card, and now she had a dinner party and a setting to die for. 'Eat your heart out,' she said out loud, talking to all the five-star restaurants she knew existed in this city. This was better than any of them.

And then she heard the front door open and had a moment's near panic. 'What have I done?' But it settled almost before the door closed. This was Angus and Noah. Coming home to her.

'I'm out here,' she called through the open doors, and waited as Angus carried Noah out onto the balcony—and stopped dead.

Well, why wouldn't they? What she'd achieved was amazing, even if she did say so herself. Sure, her credit card was smoking, but Angus had been paying solid rent, she earned decent money, and for years her card had practically grown mould.

She'd gone for balloons. At first she'd thought something tasteful, maybe silver and white, but then she'd figured, why stop there? She was making a statement and she'd gone the whole hog. There were now balloons attached to every available niche—silver, gold, crimson, white—and every crimson one had white hearts, and every white one had crimson hearts.

The party people had had suggestions of their own. They'd erected a silver pole from the centre of the table and streamers now stretched out in all directions, making the balcony looked like a carnival tent. They'd added masses of fairy lights that glittered and twinkled already, even though the sun wasn't yet down. As dusk deepened they'd be spectacular.

Who was she kidding? They were spectacular now.

And the table...

'You have no idea of the take-out options in Sydney...'

She'd pretty much explored them all. The restaurant she'd finally contacted had first been bemused, and then—when they'd realised how prepared she was to sizzle that account—they'd become enthusiastic. They'd sent their people. They'd even provided their own personal florist.

The table was set with white linen. There were sprays of frangipani, matched by vases of frangipani in the background. There was gleaming silverware and glittering white plate.

She'd tossed up whether to have table service—the idea of having waiters working seamlessly in the background sort of appealed—but then this was...a family night? Plates of prepared food were therefore warming in the oven, or crammed into the refrigerator. Canapés were already set on the table, slivers of seafood, pâtés, oysters plated on beds of ice.

A bowl of cocktail frankfurters sat in the middle of the table, sitting on a warmer because it had seemed essential that they were on display from the start. The little red sausages were Noah's favourite and they were important because this was…well, this was family and Noah was family. Wasn't he?

He would be if she had her signals right. If Angus did indeed want her.

They were here now. She stood in the background and watched their faces as they saw what was before them. Noah's eyes were like saucers. Angus's face was rigid. Expressionless.

What?

'Welcome home,' she managed.

'Is this our farewell dinner?' Angus asked tightly and she got it.

Just because she'd strung balloons with hearts…it could mean anything.

She thought again of that banner flying from the back of the plane. *Jessie, will you marry me?* It could have been meant for anyone. Any Jessie.

And hearts? You sent a heart to those you loved, but that love could be any type of love. Gratitude love. Friendship love. Affection.

'I thought it might be an anniversary dinner,' she said, cautiously, because for some reason the words were really hard to get out.

'Anniversary?'

'This date going forward,' she said, trying to

make her voice steady. 'I figured we might like to celebrate it now.'

'Why?

This was so hard—but then, suddenly it wasn't. She'd thought she might fail at the last minute, but now, watching his face…

He looked like a man who was expecting to be slapped, she realised, and with that the last of her doubts fell away.

Angus had been trained in the school of hard knocks. He'd been taught that love was conditional, eked out with reluctance and then withdrawn.

And yet he wanted her. He'd reached out to her, and it was up to her to return that courage in spades.

'I've wasted so much time,' she told him. She was standing beside the balcony railing, using it for support. He was on the far side of the table, holding Noah, who was still staring in awe at the decorations. 'I've had two whole months when I could have done this. Angus, I have a gift for you.'

'A gift…' He seemed bemused, stunned.

She signalled to a roll of paper on the table. 'This is yours, if you want it,' she said.

His eyes were still on hers, questioning, but she looked down at the paper.

He slid Noah down. The little boy walked from

balloon to balloon, uttering little crows of delight. Angus lifted the roll of paper and unwound it.

It was a house plan. A large house plan. She'd had it stored in a file on her phone, the original plan for her house back in Shearwater. She'd copied it to send to a builder when she'd arranged for the house to be divided.

She'd made a phone call today to a drafting company. She'd emailed the file. She'd made her credit card smoke some more, and an hour ago a pimply youth had delivered the scaled-up plan, rolled and tied.

She watched as Angus untied it. Looked at it. Looked at her. A question.

Say it.

Now.

'I think I love you,' she told him.

'You think?'

Deep breath. 'No. That's wrong,' she told him. 'Because I know I love you.' Then, as he still didn't move, she fought to find words to explain.

'Angus, I'm not sure if after my cowardice you still want me, but if you do…that's the original plan for my house. For *our* house if you want. It's the plan before I divided it. The plan with all barriers down. Angus, it's a house that could be ours for the rest of our lives.'

'You're saying…'

This was the hardest part. This was the part

where the guy was supposed to go down on bended knee, but how unfair was that?

'I need an aeroplane with a banner saying, *"Angus, will you marry me?"*' she babbled, and then she took a deep breath. 'But then the wrong Angus might get the message, and for me there's only one Angus. So I need to say it myself. Angus…and Noah, too, because how can I love one without the other? Angus and Noah Knox, I love you both. I love you right now, and if you let me then I'll love you for ever. So, Angus Knox, my one and only Angus, will you marry me?'

There was a long pause, a silence where the whole world seemed to hold its breath. A pause where she thought her heart had stopped. Please…

And then slowly, as if he was afraid that the silence might somehow shatter, Angus moved around the table and took her hands in his.

His eyes searched her face. His hands were strong and warm. His face showed…the beginning of hope.

'You'll marry me?'

'If you want. Because, Angus… I want you more than life itself.'

There was no mistaking his expression then. A blaze of joy hit her full on, an expression filled with wonder, hope and love. With a whoop of gladness he swept her into his arms and held her tight.

'You mean it?'

'I've never meant anything more.'

'You'd trust me?'

'If you can trust me.'

'Oh, Freya…' He paused, as if gathering himself. As if his world had suddenly aligned, the right way up.

'Then it would be my very great honour to marry you,' he said at last, smiling and smiling. 'It would give me the greatest joy I could possibly imagine.'

And then he kissed her.

'Snossages!' The crow of delight came from behind them. Noah had climbed up to the table and discovered his favourite food in the known universe. 'Daddy, snossages.'

'There you go,' Angus said, breaking off—just for a moment—from the very important task of kissing the woman he loved more than life itself. 'It seems I'm about to wed a woman who's just made the two of us the happiest men in the world. I wish I had a diamond, my Freya, to give you now.'

'I don't need diamonds,' she managed, before he kissed her again. 'I just need you.'

They wed in their garden, because where else could they wed? It was the place where they'd fallen in love. It was the place they intended staying for the rest of their lives.

There needed to be a few tweaks. The garden wasn't large enough to hold every islander who wanted to be there, and most of the islanders did. This was *their* Freya, marrying *their* doctor, and if that wasn't an excuse for the biggest celebration the island had ever seen, they didn't know what was.

The problem was solved by cutting the fencing wire between the garden and the land sweeping down to the beach. The fence would need to be rebuilt after the wedding—one dog and one small boy needed to be kept safe. The fence posts were therefore left, but massive garlands of wildflowers camouflaged each one.

A huge marquee had been set up for the food—in case it rained, though surely it wouldn't dare rain today. Islanders had been carting crates of beer, champagne, wine and soft drinks from early morning, dumping them in vats of ice. Tables were laden with food provided by every household. The island band and choir had set up a temporary stage and sound equipment.

'I'm remembering what my marriage to Deb cost,' Angus had told Freya the night before their wedding. 'This is costing us nothing.'

'Your marriage to Deb didn't cost.' They'd been sitting on the garden swing, watching the tangerine glow of sunset over the ocean. 'It brought you Noah.'

'As yours brought you Chloe.'

'For two days.' The heartbreak was still with her, would always be with her.

'She'll be in our hearts for ever,' Angus had said softly, and he'd kissed her.

She knew Angus spoke truth. Angus spoke of Chloe as family. He'd encouraged her to bring out the photos she hadn't let herself look at since Chloe's death. They now took pride of place in their rejoined house, pride of place in their hearts.

And now was the day. Now was the time.

The island band swung into a slightly wonky version of Pachelbel's Canon, but wonkiness didn't matter. The teenage flautist had brand-new braces on her teeth, but not playing on this great occasion would have broken her heart. That was unthinkable on such a day, and what did a little wonkiness matter? Angus and Freya could see no reason why everyone shouldn't share their joy.

Lily was Freya's matron of honour. Noah was ring bearer and Angus's best man. All around them were people they loved, and who loved them.

Noah had started going to the island kindergarten two days a week, and his little friends were strewing rose petals for Freya to walk on. Noah was scooting down to join them and then stumping back to stand by his dad. Proud as punch.

Robbie Veitch was sitting up the front with his mum. His job was to hold tight to a freshly washed and brushed Seaweed, and he was taking his duties seriously. Both man and dog looked content.

With Irene taking a prudent 'break' from the island, Betty now had rosters, volunteers to keep Robbie safe when she needed time to herself. The pair had never seemed happier.

Freya's Uncle Gary was beaming as well. His leg and jaw had healed well. He'd been a little put out at not being asked to give his niece away, but he'd magnanimously brought his new, state-of-the-art tractor—with roll bar—to mow the grass on the far side of the fence. His tractor just happened to remain parked where his fellow farmers could admire it, and he was one happy man.

Wilma and Fred Canning were there as well. Wilma had decreed she be in charge of catering, and had been bossing islanders around for weeks. Fred had set up the marquee. Wilma and Fred were important, they were busy, they were happy.

As were all their guests. Maureen and her husband from Sydney. Marc and Elsa from Gannet Island. So many happy people.

But not as happy as Freya.

Maureen had helped her shop in Sydney before she came home, and they'd found the dress of Freya's dreams. Made of soft, floating chiffon, with all the colours of the rainbow swirling to her feet, it was the perfect dress for a perfect day. As the music swelled she stood on the veranda looking out to where Angus stood under the arch of Scent from Heaven, and she felt as if her heart might burst.

'Ready?' Lily whispered.

'I'm ready.'

'You're loved, my dear,' Lily told her. 'Not just by Angus, but by all of us.'

'And I love you all back,' Freya managed, and then she caught Angus's smile, a smile that held so much. Oh, Angus.

'The whole island has my heart,' she whispered. 'But Angus… Angus is a part of me.'

'Then you'd better get married,' Lily said firmly—so that was what they did.

* * * * *

If you enjoyed this story, check out these other great reads from Marion Lennox

Mistletoe Kiss with the Heart Doctor
Pregnant Midwife on His Doorstep
Rescued by the Single Dad Doc
Second Chance with Her Island Doc

All available now!